"And yet, you are one of them."

"Yes," I replied. "I am one of them."

"Why, may I ask?"

"Because I was powerless to stop myself."

"You have studied atheism, agnosticism, pantheism, no doubt

rely.

Each serves

no cla

the re

larly

ridicu

this

quite

crete

evide

g?"

HELLBENT
for ELECTION

HELLBENT
for ELECTION

P. Speshock

ZONDERVAN PUBLISHING HOUSE

GRAND RAPIDS   MICHIGAN

HELLBENT FOR ELECTION
Copyright 1964 by
Zondervan Publishing House
Grand Rapids, Michigan

First printing.....September, 1964 — 8,000
Second printing.....October, 1964 — 5,000

Library of Congress Catalog Card No. 64-22829

Printed in the United States of America

To
VICTOR M. MATTHEWS
who introduced me to apologetics

PREFACE

I DO NOT INTEND to reveal the process by which the following manuscript came to be mine. Nor (since I have no way of proving otherwise) do I submit it as anything other than entirely fictional (true though some of its content *does* seem). My own personal agreement or disagreement with the characters' traits, actions, or opinions is neither here nor there. The basic point seemed to me to be that, since this saint's experiences are far different from any I have ever had (or known anyone else to have had), he is in a position to present in a fresh way the basic Christian belief which Paul stated so simply and well in his letter to the Ephesians: "For by grace are ye saved *through faith:* and that not of yourselves: it is the gift of God: Not of works, lest any man should boast."

I came to the conclusion that I am perpetually prone to losing sight of God's infinitely gigantic realm, awareness and power. I am equally prone to losing sight of my own insignificance, narrowness and meanness. I need to be shown a quality of life transcending laws, rules, regulations, ordinances and personalities, so that I might abide *within all* without consciousness of *any.* However fantastic this man's story seems, I did find my own faults pointed out to me.

It is for this reason that I decided to pass the work on for publication. I trust all who read it will bear in mind the strange circumstances of its existence and will add to them one small personal observation. We Christians disagree because we first have something in common. In that way we are like fractions — divisible because we have a Common Denominator.

HELLBENT
for ELECTION

CHAPTER 1

THE TRANSITION WAS IMMEDIATE. I was, at the one instant, writhing in my bed beneath a circlet of pale, troubled faces and, in the last half of the same, in the outer office of the High Registrar. I seemed to be seated, and yet I had no body. There were other Presences like myself in the room — which was no room at all, only space. I could not see them, and yet I knew they were there.

The one seated at my left turned to me and said, "There are three ahead of you. You will have to wait your turn."

"Yes," I said. "I know." I did not know how I knew. I only knew. I also knew their personalities and what they had appeared to be on Earth.

Across from me sat Mrs. Snob. "I hope," she said irritably, "my glorified body will have no wings. I am allergic to feathers. I would abhor the odor and upkeep. And how should my robes hang?"

Next to her, Complete Trust smothered a grin — though he had no face. "You will not have wings," he said with assurance. "Nor will you have any of the old physical problems."

She sighed heavily. "I detest waiting. I have always detested waiting. I hope I will be assigned to the nicer section — with Presences more my own type. I mean no offense," she added quickly. "However, you were a custodian, weren't you?"

11

"I was a janitor," he said with directness — and some amusement.

She sighed again. "My husband owned a small factory." And then, "Look, since you do not seem to mind the waiting and suspense as much as I do, although you were here first, I wonder — "

The Presence seated next to me said sternly, "You must take your proper turn!"

I glanced at him — though I had no eyes. His name was Rigid Pharisee. This time, I sighed.

He did not notice. He only leaned closer and hissed in my ear — which was no ear at all, "Lawbreakers! Wait until they get inside! Wait until they receive their assignments! That fluttering peahen! Can't you see she's broken every rule in the church covenant? Can't you? Can't you?"

I had the sensation of taking a deep breath. "Yes," I said. "I can see."

"Imagine!" he snorted. "The smell of smoke in this place!"

"Yes," I said. "Imagine." What I was really trying to imagine was what it might be like not to be in this place at all. . . .

But then he went on, "And that fatuous fool, Complete Trust! How often I have seen his kind with their sweet smiles and their nodding heads and their 'leave-them-to-the-Lord' philosophy! Don't they know the brethren must be corrected? Don't they know the stronger of us — "

But suddenly the outer office seemed expanded. Invisible chairs appeared and were at once filled with young Presences. I knew, with no one telling me, that they had been a youth group on their way to a rally.

The Receptionist materialized from the mist surrounding the desk at the end of the office. "Mr. Trust, come this way . . ." The voice was high and clear. The garb was long and luminous. The face was clearly defined and expression-less. They disappeared behind the great white iridescent door.

12

There was a rustle among the young Presences. Rigid Pharisee named them aloud. "Saved By Faith Without Understanding. What a pity they hadn't longer to warrant this reward."

Mrs. Snob moved across to sit at my right. "Children upset me," she said. "And what was that Receptionist? Male or female?"

"Up here," I heard myself saying, "that is of no importance."

Rigid Pharisee approved of this. "Aha! I see you have read the Gospels! This is good! This is good! It is more," he added, leaning around me toward Mrs. Snob, "than I can say for *you!*" If he had had a finger, I felt sure he would have pointed it.

She drew her bodiless form erect. "Weren't you," she said coldly, "some kind of brick*lay*er who fancied himself a *lay* preacher?"

"I," he said fiercely, "was a man of God! Ill-health kept me from schooling, but never forget that He Who sitteth at the right hand of the Father began His physical life as a carpenter's Son!"

"Mmm," she mused. "I've wondered about that . . ."

But then the Receptionist was before her. "Mrs. Snob, come this way . . ." And they were gone, with only the click of the huge gold latch behind them.

"She'll get hers," Pharisee chuckled. "I hope they assign her to my mansion. I'll see she's purged!"

There was another restless movement among the young Presences, and suddenly a very old Presence was seated beside me. Her name, I knew immediately, was Mrs. Insecure.

"I made it," she said with conspicuous non-existent tears. "I never read the Book all the way through, you see, and at the last minute I had some doubt."

"Probably skipped Leviticus!" Pharisee snorted.

"I wonder if my husband will be here," she continued, a

13

tremor in her voice. "He was a small man. Slight Skeptic was his name. I don't suppose you've —"

"No," I said. "We've just arrived ourselves."

"Probably not here," Pharisee said with conviction. "Doesn't deserve to be if he spent his time doubting."

But then the Receptionist was standing before him. "Mr. Pharisee, come this way . . ."

He arose and I imagined for a second that he tried to give me a reassuring wink. "I'll put in a good word for you," he said. Though he was indistinguishable, I could see him swaggering.

Mrs. Insecure fidgeted along with the young Presences, but for a different reason. "I don't like that creature," she said, "that Rigid Pharisee. His kind was half the cause of my husband's doubting. In the first place, there were science and history. But in the second place, why believe if it turned you into one of *those?*"

"Yes," I said, "I understand."

"You seem like a nice sort," she said then. "Not at all opinionated. It's difficult to believe of you."

"What is difficult to believe of me?"

"That your name could be what it is."

"Oh," I said. And then the Receptionist stood before me. "Mr. Hellbent, come this way . . ."

CHAPTER 2

THE HIGH REGISTRAR WAS of a decided male semblance. His face, though youthfully beardless, was corrugated by age. Ruddy, yet somber. His hair was a hoary hood. His apparel cascaded in the same silvery luminescence and was trimmed with gold. The desk behind which he sat was overlaid with gold. The space designated as his office seemed to be bounded on all sides by shimmering, indistinct whiteness.

He waited until I had finished ogling the place and then said, "You are Mr. Hellbent? Mr. Willfully Hellbent?" He glanced at a scroll unfurled on his desk, but I recognized that as a red herring. He knew all of the answers. It was a type of psychology intended to make obvious my errors through my own replies.

Nonetheless, he held the upper hand. "I am he," I said.

"Please be seated," he said. "And give, if you can, justification for your name, in a single sentence."

I settled myself weightlessly and answered, "The justification for my name is simply that I harbor no desire to spend eternity with Believers."

His eyes were clear and cold and pierced to the immaterial depths of me. "That," he said, "was explanation, not justification."

I pondered this for a moment. "Do you mean," I asked,

"that I must define the just causes for my lack of desire to spend eternity with Believers?"

He nodded. "Now you're getting the idea."

"I suppose you must know this in order to classify and assign me?"

"That's some of it. Truth is more of it."

"Well, then," I said, "the just causes for my lack of desire to spend eternity with Believers are the Believers themselves — their behavior and determined ignorance of it."

"And yet," he said, scanning the scroll again, "you are one of them."

"Yes," I replied. "I am one of them."

"Why, may I ask?"

"Because I was powerless to stop myself."

"You were a scribe," said he.

"Yes. You could call it that."

"You must then have read a great deal?"

"Yes. A great deal."

"You have studied atheism, agnosticism, pantheism, no doubt? Did none of these convince you?"

"Certainly not! You have all that in my record, surely. Each one defeated itself. A thing with no beginning deserves no claim to a middle or an ending. That which appeals to the reason should at least be reasonable."

He nodded. "I take it evolution seemed particularly ridiculous to you, then?"

"Particularly."

"Idealism? You explored that, too?"

"I did. As with all analyses of speculations, I found this quite unsatisfying."

"I take it you could not settle for less than concrete evidence."

"That's right."

"You feel Christianity affords this?"

"I do."

"Christianity has a beginning, a middle and an ending?"

16

"It has."

"And the mysteries do not deter you?"

"They do not. They will be explained. Already, this office and you are more clearly obvious."

"Yes," he said. "You are right."

"How will you classify me?" I asked.

He frowned slightly. "I could classify you as most anything and assign you to most any post," he said, "and you could be made to be perfectly happy. That is the nature of this place."

"I realize this," I said.

He looked at me piercingly again. "Why then do you choose to ignore the future harmony of your coexistence with Believers?"

"There are degrees or, to be specific 'rewards,' in this place, I understand? Decided upon by the vice or virtue inflicted by one's self into the central core, or soul?"

"New Nature is prevalent," he said.

"But qualities cultivated on Earth determine our status here?"

He sighed. "I can see that you will need counseling."

"Counseling!" I snorted. "You do that? Up here?"

"Do not forget," he said, "that you are here by a decision to believe and accept. It could have been done otherwise. You could be made happy by other means, but that is not our characteristic."

He set about jotting notes with a golden quill on what looked to be a prescription pad. When he had finished, he tore off the sheet and handed it to me. I could see that the lettering, which was unlike any human language I had ever looked upon, was also in gold.

I started to say, "I have no hands — " But the glimmering wisp affixed itself to my front, like a note pinned to a school boy! I could not help laughing.

"I am tagged Nothingness!" I said.

He arose and held up a finger. "Ah, no!" he said. "Up

17

here, you are important. You have always been important to Him. Even before you existed down there."

I felt a moment of shame. "I wish I did not rebel," I mumbled. "But even up here – in the outer office – they irked me."

"The Presences in the outer office were friendly to you."

"Of course!" I grunted. "They misunderstood my name to mean that I was altogether worldly. They badger only the church-attending brethren. They befriend the worldly. They are attracted to him. They invite him to evangelistic meetings and pray for him. It is only *after* he has become one of them that they set about tormenting him!"

He shook his head. "The outer office is only the first step in the transformation, Hellbent. You were misled by what they *appeared* to be on Earth – and by their gibberish. Do not forget what they actually are: Believers. This is what counts."

My mouth and my fists wanted to tighten. "I have told myself this for ten years on Earth," I said evenly, "and I have borne every second of the knowledge like a heavy yoke. The sum total of it is this: believing is *all* they have in common – mere believing!"

His eyes were now compassionate. "If I did not know that all things are under His jurisdiction, or if I in any way felt tempted to abuse my free will to the end of reasoning, I would be inclined to deduce that yours was an untimely transition. However, to reason against Illimitable Knowledge would be the pinnacle of witless wickedness, and I have no wish to indulge. It does remain that you are not yet ready for this place."

"Perhaps," I said hopefully, "I will never be ready. Perhaps I am some little blunder slithered out from between the fingers of a demon."

And now he chuckled. "You are no blunder," he said. "I have it all here." And he patted the scroll. "Nonetheless, in lieu of alteration by Divine Power invested in me, I am referring you to the Chief Counselor."

CHAPTER 3

THE WORDS WERE NO SOONER spoken than I stood in the office of the Chief Counselor. The offices were identical, but the Chief Counselor's face was blurry and his garment trimmed with tarnished silver. He looked strangely out of place.

"That was done in a twinkling," I said. "I suppose procedures quicken as we become able to accept the non-existence of Time?"

"Quite right." The voice was masculine-sounding.

"And do you take these forms simply to be symbolic? For our benefits?"

"Right again."

"And the fact that your face is not clearly discernible indicates that I have taken a step backward, instead of forward?"

"Yes."

"And the silver is exchanged for gold to show that I am close to forfeiting the more precious?"

"Very perceptive, Hellbent."

"Why, then, is the note affixed to me?"

"A reminder, Hellbent, that your heart is to be that of a child, even if your head is not."

I laughed. "But I have neither! I shed them down below. By now, my former veins are filled with formaldehyde!"

"I was speaking of the will to love and of intelligence,

Hellbent. I used the heart and head as symbols, so that you could understand."

I sobered considerably. "Sorry," I mumbled.

"It appears that you have more tendency to humor now that you are certain of eternity than when you were probing about in the possibility that the grave was the utter end of you. Be seated."

"Yes, sir."

"Now, then." And the note was gone from me and seemed, somehow, to have gotten on his desk. "We need not go through the great claptrap of getting you to recognize your problem. You have already voiced it. You have no wish to dwell eternally with Believers. Are you certain the motivation for this lies not in any grudge against Christianity itself?"

I smiled faintly. "You seem to have absorbed a good bit of the Socratic method up here."

I thought for a second his eyes became very clear and sharp. "Or he of ours," he snapped. "But stick to the issue."

"I have no 'grudge' exactly against Christianity. Certainly no argument."

"Which means?"

"Which means I have believed and accepted it, but do not particularly like the condition as regards my so-called 'brethren.'"

He grunted. "Are you honestly so foolhardy as to think conditions happier in hell?"

"That would depend upon one's definition of happiness. If one sought only comfort, then no. But if one sought peace, then yes."

"Great sordid blasphemy!" he cried. "You dare say that? Up here? You dare question the state of peace?"

"I do not question the state of peace," I said. "I only maintain that it must have come about by force — which is no peace at all. Extremely few of the Believers I knew progressed far enough to live in mutual loving peace, without pretense."

20

"Would you expect us to refuse admission to those without perfect qualifications?"

"Of course not. Nor do you. I simply said I do not have the stomach to live with them. In fact," I grinned, "I have no stomach at all . . ."

"Stop being asinine, Hellbent. This is more serious than you think. Once condemned to hell, you could not howl and come back up here. And, once condemned to hell, you would certainly find no inhabitants with 'mutual loving peace,' either!"

"But, sir," I said, "there is peace where there is no expectation. If you know that all is evil and torture and you expect nothing more, this is a kind of peace. Each glimmering of alleviation would become a ray of happiness. Whereas, if you are surrounded by good resulting from repressed evil and underdeveloped loving-kindness, the anticipation of sudden thrusts of cruelty would be unbearable. To me, at least."

"You have a low esteem of Christian behavior."

"I have a low esteem of *Believers'* behavior."

"But you have no doubt of Who holds the reins?"

"No doubt whatever."

"And you dare anticipate 'sudden thrusts of cruelty' from Believers up here? You dare suggest repressed evil exists here?"

His countenance seemed brighter but, somehow, more ominous. I felt myself wishing he would say, "Fear not." But still I plunged on, as bravely as I could, "I seem to recall the sin of pride. I seem to recall that Lucifer —"

"Was cast *down!*" he roared. And suddenly there appeared in his hand a drawn sword! His visage was dark and dreadful in extreme contrast to the glare of his raiment. I wanted to back away, but I was hypnotized by a realization.

"He is not God's opposite at all!" I heard myself saying. "He is only one of *you* — gone bad . . ."

"Absolutely! And you dally with the thought of joining his forces?"

"But surely," I said, "as your desire is to be away from

21

him, so is my desire to be separated from those of my kind whose tactics I loathe. He was cast out, but I must commingle eternally. I do not justify the actions of my opposites, unbelievers. I only contend that there is innocence where evil abounds, and a surety of evil where innocence is a pretext."

He thrust the sword away in a gesture of impatience and it disappeared. Then he sat down behind the desk and twiddled his thumbs. "Relax, Hellbent," he said. And then I understood that all his action had been therapeutic.

"Apparently," I said with apology, "I am beyond redemption by logic or fear."

"Apparently," he said.

"Apparently I will need some claptrap of talking it out. Or else expulsion. My belief has placed me in a strange predicament."

"We are used to strange predicaments," he said. "Nothing is impossible up here. The ticklish part lies in effecting a cure involving your free will. Before assigning you to an Individual Counselor, I should like to clarify one point. Exactly what, in your estimation, is 'Believers' behavior'? Do you class it as behavior which pleases Believers?"

"No, sir. Not at all. I class it as behavior which will preserve Christianity."

"Christian behavior is the ideal which Believers' behavior feigns?"

"Yes, sir. Precisely. And evil is most successful masqueraded as shallow piety."

"Better, then, to be outwardly, admittedly evil?"

"Yes, sir. For I sincerely believe the imprints made upon the central core to be less ugly for a sin already discovered and expiated on Earth than for one stealthily concealed or, worse yet, disguised as righteousness."

"You are saying that many good people go to hell and many bad ones come up here?"

"Too many, both ways."

22

"And mere belief is the hinge which swings them the one way or the other?"

"Yes, sir."

He took a deep breath. "I can see that your Individual Counselor will jolly well need a briefing." But I noted for the first time a twang of mirth.

CHAPTER 4

I WAS THEN SUDDENLY ALONE in space. In the far, far distance I could see the recurrent glint of gold, like the faint, unsteady gleam of a sunrise on a cloudy day. A chill of desolation swept through me. But as I strained to scan the horizon there appeared walking toward me a man garbed all in white with rays of phosphorescence flickering off in his wake. As he came nearer I could see that there was no trim at all on his mantle, only the radiance. His features were unclouded and common except for the keen perception of the eyes. In Earth-years, he looked to be approximately in his mid-fifties. His arrival instilled a sense of relief.

"You do not look," I said, "as if you needed a briefing."

He smiled. "The Chief likes to make jokes," he said, "when he knows all the solutions."

"Oh," I said. "Do you know all the solutions?"

"No," he said. "Not I."

"Then you are not omniscient?"

"Oh, no. We are ministering spirits sent out to minister for those who shall be heirs of salvation. Our knowledge extends as far as our ministering requires."

"I am an 'heir of salvation'?"

"You are. But you don't want to be, I take it?"

I sighed. We seemed to be walking along together. That is, I followed along at his side.

"Must I defend my position to you, too?" I asked. "Surely you have all that information?"

"It was in your dossier. You regard as true and factual the doctrines of Christianity, which constitutes belief and acceptance, but you feel that the lack of competition and comparison in hell would likewise constitute a sort of peace and contentment. Has it not occurred to you that the demons might well be vying for personal betterment and, in the scuffle, feed upon your agony?"

"My agony," I said, "would at least be perpetual, and their vying should be their own unhappy fluctuation. But, tell me, don't we seem to be going away from the golden glimmer?"

"That we do, Hellbent. When you say that your agony would be perpetual, must you not also concede that your status up here would be the same?"

"Why, no! Because down there the agony would override all other drives. Up here, timelessness must give allowance for mischief as with Sat—"

"I know, I know," he said quickly. "Please don't mention that rotter's name to me! Let's be done with defenses for now and get on with the business at hand. You may call me Alexis, if you like, since we shall migrate conjointly for a season."

"Migrate?" I asked. "Then I am being expelled?" I turned and the glimmer had completely disappeared. We seemed lost in an expanse of distant blue shading into gray. Alexis was the only bright spot.

"Eventually perhaps," he said, not slowing his pace a step to wait for me. "Right now we are on our way to Earth."

I stopped short. *"Earth!"* I recalled that the High Registrar had felt my transition was untimely.

"Earth," he said quietly, continuing to walk.

"Like *this*?" I danced about trying to indicate my incorporeity.

"Settle down, Hellbent," he said. "Not to live, just to prove your case." And he kept up that spritely pace.

25

"Are we to walk all the way?" I asked, getting out of patience with the whole situation.

"The walk," he said, "is to acquaint us. You should have figured that out. Besides, you're quite a few thousand years younger than I am." And now he twinkled in my direction.

"Oh," I said, beginning to get the drift of things again. "You selected this countenance to suggest the father image?"

"Hardly father," he said. "More uncle, I think."

"So that I will believe you and trust your judgment?"

"Something like that."

"But — won't they see you on Earth? Glowing like that?"

He chuckled. "Hardly! They never seem to see us. Surely you remember how it was with Balaam?"

I thought for a minute and then laughed aloud. "I remember now. The ass saw the angel before the prophet did!"

"Exactly, Hellbent. Doesn't say much for your vision, does it? I suspect that even the best of you has a trace of Sadducee in him. But then, it is not in my sphere to suspect."

"What will we do," I asked then, "when we get to earth? May I visit my grave and see what they have done with that end of me?"

"Vanity, vanity," he muttered. "Why do we not start at the other end of things?"

"The other end of things?"

"Your birth."

"My *birth!*"

"Great thunder, Hellbent! Were you a man or a parrot? Of course your birth. What you are evolves out of what you were. Haven't you harped singularly upon that since your arrival? We will take it a step farther and go back to what you were before you became a Believer."

I wanted to scowl. "If you intend to prove that the Believer is what he is because of what he was before, then I will not be likely to swallow it. The doctrine of Christianity is, in itself, an education and imbues the Believer with wisdom and susceptibility to change and expanse. I will not be hoodwinked into sickish sentimentality by the unearthing of a sluggish or tyrannical parent!"

"Ah, Hellbent," he sighed. "Given your heads, what noise-makers you children of redemption become. Have I said that I am here to make excuses for your brethren? Or to debate with you the subject of judging?"

"Judging!" I bellowed. "Do not forget that the function of a judge is also to hand down sentence. Nor expect my belief to render me so inhibited that I am unable to exercise my critical faculties nor voice simple truth nor confront those of my own kind openly and without fear of sin. We have a Guide Book. Am I to become mealy-mouthed, imbedded in falsehood, because my fellows accumulate and practice unlimited miasmic supposition?"

"Bravo!" he said. "I believe we are reaching the point of descent. Are you ready, Hellbent?"

And it was then that I knew that I had been baited again.

"Quite," I said. "The sooner we get done with me, the better."

CHAPTER 5

WE STOOD AT ONCE before a small frame house in the ratty end of a Midwest village.

"This is where you were born, Hellbent?" Alexis asked — although of course he already knew.

"Yes," I said. "And quite a hygienic birth it was, coming at the closing of the midwife era and before the conception of socialized medicine and the periodic pilgrimages to the hospital. It was no small mark of privilege to have been delivered by a doctor. This was then the better end of town, you see. Fine old houses near the business district. Before the exodus to suburbia."

"Would you like to go in and browse about?" he asked.

"No," I said, watching two Pygmy-sized ragamuffins frolic on the grassless dust with a burry mongrel. "I think not."

"Do you recall anything of living here?"

"No. Only that I have been told of the place and have had it pointed out to me. We moved from here when I was just past two."

"Well, then," he said. "Let us not dawdle."

"Shall we walk?" I asked. "It isn't far. Perhaps half a mile to my second home."

He sent me an amused glance. "I say, Hellbent, for a creature so steamed against sentimentality you do have a mawkishness over the past. I dare venture the High Registrar was correct in his analysis of you. But don't worry. You'll see enough of this place before we're through."

Presently we stood on the broad green lawn of the suburban farm where I had lived to young manhood. The house was large and square and plain. The farm, now worked, had been then a wilderness of enchantment through which Della and I had romped and roamed and hidden and dreamed. For a fleeting instant I fancied that I could hear again Della's airy laughter as she ran through the fields with her white legs quite scratched and disreputable and her black hair flowing out behind her like a wild stallion's mane. I could see her leaping and galloping, ahead of me all the time and delighted over it, and falling at last to a breathless ragged heap on the hill beneath the gnarled little crab apple tree. "I," she would say, waving her skinny young arms dramatically, "shall be quite wicked when I grow up! None of this religion for me! For wickedness begets good just as good begets wickedness . . ."

"Tell me about her," Alexis said. "Tell me about Della."

I nodded, feeling sadness. "Della is my sister," I said. "Five minutes my senior and filled, as a child, with mystery and knowledge transfused from the public library, wisdom and disillusion drawn from our circumstances. Della was only her nickname. Her proper name was Deliberately."

"I see," he said. "Deliberately Hellbent. What became of her?"

I drew a long breath. "She grew," I said. "She became a beautiful woman, cold and determined. She married. Her husband's name is Non Regenerate. A fine fellow. Hard-working and upstanding. Practices moderation. Never argues politics or religion. Good name in the community. Never maudlin or fuddled. Knows where he's going."

"I dare say," Alexis mumbled. "But before you began talking about her, you were thinking about her. You were remembering a thing she said as a child. 'Wickedness begets good as good begets wickedness.' Have you any idea what she meant by that?"

"Of course," I said. "She meant our parents. She watched wickedness grow out of good and she felt, as I do, that where wickedness prevails good must eventually come from it. If you have gone down as far as far is, then you must out of necessity either stabilize or rise up. The stabilization is good because it has reached the depths of bad and can get no worse. The rising up is decided improvement and happiness."

"Marrying Non Regenerate, it does not seem as if she fared so badly?" he suggested.

"Of course not. There is the proof of her theory."

"But what wickedness grew out of what good regarding your parents?"

"Well," I said, "in the beginning they were both very, very good. They came from very, very good families. They belonged to very, very good churches. They were, in fact, distant cousins. There was no need for my mother to change her name when she married my father. Her name was Vex Hellbent, and his name was Taunt Hellbent. The problem arose out of all this very, very goodness. You see, they belonged to different churches. Now, one of them, they decided, must be the *right one*. But *which* one? She argued for her denomination. He argued for his. Her relatives came every Wednesday and argued her defense. His relatives came every Friday and argued his. Soon they were not speaking, except on Wednesdays and Fridays when everyone shouted. Soon after that, they were not sleeping together. They wrangled about divorce as they wrangled about all else. They disregarded the Guide Book altogether, that *It* regards the marriage union a contract covering a lifetime and that severance of such contract is no less than an outrage and should be resorted to only under extreme conditions and subject to continued continence thereafter, *providing* both members of the marriage, or both halves of the one body, are Believers. My parents were Believers."

"There is an exception," he mused.

"Ah, yes!" I said. "And I know that exception. But no

30

fornication had occurred here. At the time the subject came under debate, there was only hateful restraint."

"They divorced, then?"

"Not at all! Not for years!"

"But if they waived religious regulation, what was the impediment?"

"There were two: Della and I. Though, by this time, they had begun to cast about wondering how they had got us at the start. And it *was* still a denominational tangle. For, you see, she would not have us reared in his church and he would not have us be reared in hers. We were, therefore, reared alternately in both — for as long as it lasted."

"And how did it terminate?"

"With Della's rebellion. At the age of seventeen she ran off and married Non Regenerate."

"And your parents did not have this annulled?"

"Of course not. It was the escape both had longed for. Oh, they ranted mildly on 'mixed marriage,' implying that Della was a Believer, but I recall that she answered them quite smartly. By this time she was sassing off to them at regular intervals. I recall that she tossed her head and yipped back, 'If I started out from this moment on with but one goal in mind, that of making a mess of my life, I could in no way hope for the success you've flaunted these many years! Never mention your beliefs to me again! I am sick to vomiting over your measly arguments on wine, water, vestments, sabbaths and the whole lot! I am positively, absolutely and irrevocably *finished* with religion!' And she went to her husband's side and cleaved."

"And your parents?" he asked. "What became of them?"

"Oh, they threw both religions out the window, divorced, remarried, moved off, and I haven't seen them since."

"And *their* relatives? Each so determined to be right?"

I chuckled. "That's strange, too," I said. "His relatives joined her church, and her relatives joined his."

"And you, Hellbent? What mark did this leave on you?"

"Well," I said slowly, "I decided that none of them could be wholly accurate. I decided that if there is a God at all, He could not be confined by any one set of boundaries or condensed into one neat little package and made available only to a single group. He must be Huge — and belong to anyone who seeks Him. But of course at the time I knew only that I was homeless, and that Non Regenerate offered me a place at my twin's side — food, clothing and shelter."

CHAPTER 6

WE HAD BY NOW WALKED to the back of the farm, to the hill upon which the crab apple tree stood, and had settled ourselves to watch the coral sun withdraw and give license to the cooling breeze which straightway shared a dozen secrets with even rows of twittering young corn.

"I don't wonder," Alexis said, "that your species becomes attached to this place. Considering all things, it was mighty big of Him to leave you as much of Eden as He did. But then, you had just concluded at the age of seventeen that He must be Huge, hadn't you? Getting back to the years between, I take it your earliest recollections were of your twin sister and your parents. Can you think what your next most poignant memory was?"

"Yes," I said. "Della and I had a dog. He was killed by a truck. We must have been about four. His name was Escape. After he died and we understood that if we replaced him the same thing would likely happen again, living so close to the road, there was nothing left but to observe the antics of people."

"I see," he said. "And what was your first memory of this sort, then?"

I felt embarrassed. "You will laugh, Alexis."

"Not at all. Say on."

"Well, this may seem foreign to you. Since, when you take on the human form, apparently you don't —"

"Streaks of lightning, Hellbent, get to the point!"

"Well — I remember the belching."

"*Belching?*" he questioned.

"Belching, Alexis."

"Can you mean ejecting wind from the stomach through the mouth?"

"Precisely."

"But wasn't that a rather strange antic, Hellbent?"

"Della and I thought so, too, Alexis. I suppose that is why we were so enthralled."

"But *who,* for the sake of nonsense — "

"It was not nonsense, Alexis. And it was the Shepherd of my mother's church — "

"Buffoon!" he cried. "Let's not waste time on the ludicrous!"

"I swear, Alexis, it's the truth."

"Ah, ah," he said. "Swear not at all. But if you have a serious point to make, I am obliged to listen. How was it, then?"

"Well, the Shepherd of my mother's church and the Shepherd of my father's church took turns coming to Sunday dinner. Now, this was while they each still attended church, prior to the time I was five. That is, Della and I. Now, the Shepherd of my mother's church was a round, red shiny man who flattered her cooking and ate until he emitted a roseate glow. It was most beautiful to see. He had silver hair and bright blue eyes. He wore a black suit and a very white shirt. When he had finished eating at last, he would say, 'As long as I am with my family . . . You *are* my family, you know, one and all . . .' And then he would unfasten his belt and loosen his tie and pat his stomach and belch wonderfully and make jokes about 'his favorite indoor sport.' Mama was always pleased and laughed softly. 'Delightful man,' she said. 'Marvelous sense of humor.' And then he would arise to his feet and do his imitation."

"Imitation?" Alexis asked. "What sort of imitation?"

34

"Well, sir, first he pretended to be smoking. He took long drags on an imaginary cigarette and rocked back on his heels and pursed his lips and blew deliciously, with his eyes closed and his face upward."

"Appalling!" said Alexis. "What then?"

"Then," I said, "he staggered around the room like a very drunken man and fell, at last, onto the couch where he slept until supper. Mama always woke him in time to have a bite and be off to evening services."

"And your father?" he asked. "How did he take all this?"

"Oh, he went fishing on the Sundays Mother's Shepherd was due. He stayed home only for his own Shepherd."

"Well," Alexis sighed, "I trust *he* was more of a gentleman."

"I suppose it depends upon your point of view. You see, he liked a nip of wine with his meals — and a good cigar afterwards. He ate very little, but he wanted each thing 'just right.' Mama, who refused to cook with wine, was up for constant sneers and criticism. My father did the buying for these meals and apologized throughout for his wife's narrow-mindedness. When this Shepherd was finished eating, he took sodium bicarbonate — and a trifle more wine, 'for his stomach's sake.' He then explained over and over to Mama, who was obliged to let the dishes stand in the sink for sake of keeping holy the sabbath (when she would have preferred to keep clean the kitchen) that her form of fundamentalism was nothing more than conscience-training."

"Conscience-training, Hellbent?"

"Yes. He maintained that if she had been brought up not to eat pork, as the Israelites had, then she would necessarily have felt very guilty over the ham she served him. If she had been brought up never to cut her hair, as the Nazarites had, then she would suffer a painful attack of conscience each time she passed a mirror and saw her short bob. She would, he said, probably wear a snood until she felt it had grown to what she could consider a 'decent length.' As it was, he pointed out, she had been brought up to respect entirely the wrong restrictions."

"His church was not fundamentalist, then?"

"Oh, but it was! Decidedly!"

Alexis inclined his head. "I don't wonder that you became confused, Hellbent. Tell me, what did *you* decide from all this?"

By now the sun was gone and the evening chill set in. "I decided, Alexis, that neither was entirely right. As for the men, each of them was a glutton in his own way. The one for out-and-out gorging, and the other for picking peevishly. The sin of the one was as bad as the sin of the other. They were, in fact, the same sin turned inside-out. Though neither would go to hell for it."

"And the arguments of fundamentalism. What of those?"

"I would have thought it better to return to the Guide Book and admit to each other that no one set of rules governs Him, therefore it was idiocy to assume that either set of rules should be applicable to His subjects. Organizations must have rules, but to give the impression that their exclusive mechanism is the only one approved by Him is atrocious. And it is little wonder that each, looking upon the other, refuses to join in."

"I take it then that you concluded He is undenominational?"

"I concluded that His grace is sufficient for all and certainly capable of transcending picayunish dissimilarities."

"You learned much of churchiness at an early age, I see."

"But perhaps not enough of Him. And I concluded all this later."

"Enough to cause me to wonder why you did not change your name."

"Ah," I said, "but we have not yet come to the later parts of learning, when church attendance was banned completely and spite reigned supreme. Besides, you must have misunderstood me. I have been pointing out to you a few of the direct reasons I find your upper abode completely unenticing. How can you twist this to the end that I should have changed my name?"

"Well, yes," he said after a minute. "I was thinking that you had seen through them. I had forgotten that they had not seen through themselves. Only each other. Or so they thought. But then, it's too dark to do more tonight, and this business of lugging about a human form is fatiguing. Shall we rest here?"

"I don't mind," I said, "though I don't feel a bit sleepy. I suppose I shall rest my thoughts and be ready for you to-morrow. Does your form have weight?"

"No," he yawned. "No weight and no upkeep. Just the perpetual knowledge of its awkwardness. This is trouble enough. Goodnight, Hellbent."

"Goodnight, Alexis."

I settled myself beside him and discovered it was quite comfortable to have no body to ache and twitch and rebel over the lumpy ground.

CHAPTER 7

I WAS AROUSED BY THE SOUND of gagging and sputtering. "Pttui!" said Alexis. "Ghastly stuff!" At one glance, it was obvious what he had been about.

"They are a sour variety," I said, "and not nearly ripe."

"I wonder that Eve could have been tempted in such a fashion," he fussed. "*I* should not have been!"

"But, Alexis," I said, "you just *were* . . ."

"Nonsense," he said. "I would never have swallowed the thing. All your talk about human food yesterday aroused my curiosity, that's all. When I awoke to see the undernourished thing bobbing above me, I plucked it down solely to discover how well-founded your human ado on this subject really is. If you ask me, much ado about less than nothing."

I sighed, looking up at the morning sun. "I would of course agree with you, Alexis. Though none of my parents' relatives would."

"What have your parents' relatives to do with this now? I thought we had left them in the turnabout pursuit of each other's denomination?"

"We had, Alexis, but that was many years later — after they chiseled away at my parents' marriage until there was nothing left of it. Meantime, each group fervently followed its own teachings, with Della and me tugged back and forth between the two. That all came about after the sex, however."

"After the sex?" he asked. "Hellbent, I am here to help you, but you will have to keep to the issue at hand. First now, what of being tugged back and forth according to the teachings of each denomination?"

I drew a long breath. "Well, this is of itself a quandary. For when I say that each followed *its own* teachings, I mean exactly that. The Shepherd was hired, you see, to teach them. But, first off, he was met by a board of *their* peers and told *what* to teach them. If he showed signs of thinking for himself, he was naturally corrected. If he refused the correction, he was let out. Thus, you see, the members were taught what they wanted to be taught and heard what they wanted to hear, and the Shepherd, to be a successful fellow at all, must necessarily be very elastic. I think all this was caught up, somehow, in what you and I would call 'tradition' — a word both denominations despised because it framed a large portion of the dogma of the more formal sects. And if they disliked each other, you can see how zealously they pitted themselves against a body of worshipers holding tradition a partner with the Guide Book."

"Dear, dear," said Alexis. "But you mentioned a couple of times that they themselves did not stick to the Guide Book."

"Of course not. But the other fellow's horn always honks louder."

"To get back to the two Shepherds, though, each of them had the approval of his own flock, I take it?"

"Yes and no, Alexis. If either had been a completely headstrong fellow and sought to teach exactly what was in the Guide Book and not what they liked to *think* was in the Guide Book, then he would have been dismissed. (Or if they had tired of him and felt he had become a bore.) But since each had given the impression of agreeing, more or less, with the general lessons and only now and again sniped off a shot at them, displaying, in his own life, open shortcomings, well then he was kept on and treated in like manner. It was a sort of

39

armed truce, you see, with gossip and back-biting as the underground. But of course this was carried on between members as well as between members and Shepherd. And not all Shepherds *knew* Its true contents."

"Before we get to that," Alexis said, "let's get back to you and Della and what happened to you at the hands of the relatives. I am beginning to weary of this knot of a place."

"When we were just past five," I said, "my parents put an end to church attending. The Shepherds ceased to be invited to Sunday dinner. The Guide Books were burned. (Not that they ever read from Them, anyway.) And the relatives dropped in intermittently, waving their arms and trying to convict everyone of sin. Although Della and I were quite confused as to what 'sin' actually was. It generally boiled down to be the opposite of what *they* thought it was. At any rate, my mother's relatives said, 'Think of the children! They must go to church!' And my mother, with a gleam in her eye, said, 'Yes, indeed. Take them along.' Then my father's relatives would say, 'Think of the children! They must go to *our* church!' And my father, baring his teeth, would say, 'By all means. Take them along!' And so it was that Della and I went one Sunday to the one church and the next Sunday to the other. And since many of the teachings were quite opposite, we should have become quite insane had we attempted to absorb and practice both. The result was obviously that we set about living up to our names. We took in as little as possible and sat dreaming in the pews of an eternity excluding the whole lot of them. Which is perhaps why I choose to this day to refer to them as my parents' relatives, rather than my own. Della does likewise."

"I see," said Alexis, shifting his position. "This situation prevailed, then, from the time you were five until you were seventeen?"

"Yes, more or less. Though during the latter of those years we flared our nostrils and ran out to pasture and refused to be dragged along at all. That is, Della did. I often followed suit. We differed in this. She wanted none of churchiness at all. I kept harking back to the Guide Book, wondering just how all the gerrymandering came about."

"And what did the Guide Book say?"

"Unless I misunderstood completely, *He* was more concerned with stating the truth than with pleasantly tickling the ears of His audience. And unless I am far off the track, His audiences numbered into the several thousands, willing to walk for miles with no thought of food or cushioned compartments. When I was younger, I used to wonder how this could be. For all the proper folk would begin to open their watch cases and clear their throats and pull on their gloves when the lesson became too long. And then the Shepherd would hurriedly dismiss them."

"By and large, Hellbent," Alexis said, "you seem to have kept a level head on your shoulders and sorted all things out befittingly."

He arose and I did likewise.

"No, Alexis, I did not sort as well as you think. I speak to you now as an adult and still you feel I am in need of counseling. Think how much more in need I was as a child beset by a profusion of hate and a bounty of contradictions, and all of it born out of very, very goodness. But then, you have caused me to skip over the most confusing part of all, my next most poignant recollection."

"Not at all, Hellbent. I am taking you there now. To your mother's bedroom."

CHAPTER 8

WE STOOD IMMEDIATELY IN THE FRONT upstairs bedroom of the big square house. A housewife in a gingham dress flitted about with a feather duster, humming, giving the pillows a plump, the bottom of the bed a pat, and disappearing at last down the hallway.

"I think," I told Alexis, "that she walked right through me."

"Very possible," he said with a shrug. "You have no substance. At least none that she can realize, and she can realize only what she already knows."

"She can't hear us, either?"

"Not at all, Hellbent. She hasn't the ear to hear. So then, this was your mother's bedroom?"

I looked about the room, freshly papered now and with crisp curtains at the window. My mother had not been such a housekeeper — at least in the later years.

"This was her bedroom. Though the bed was not here against the wall but, rather, diagonally in that corner. I was six years old, I remember — "

"Yes, yes, Hellbent. Don't bog down now."

"I ran in from playing in the fields to ask whether Della and I might open the new package of cookies. (She had stopped having time for baking.) Della had teased me into doing the asking, saying that she must always be the brave

42

one and that, by rights, I should have been the girl. So she waited downstairs and I went up, two at a time, and burst into the room. . . . We had looked downstairs and called and thought she might be taking a nap — which she often did now that she had begun drinking the wine, too."

"Did it not occur to you that she would be angry if you woke her?"

"Of course. That was where the bravery came in. Only — she was not asleep at all. There was a man with her."

"Did you know the man?"

"Yes. He had started coming to the house regularly. He drank a great deal and talked a great deal and told loud, boastful stories. She had told us to call him 'Uncle,' but his real name was Thrill Chaser."

"Did she see you immediately?"

"No. Only after several seconds."

"Why did you stand there for several seconds?"

"I could not seem to move."

"Why did you not speak?"

"I had no voice."

"Did you know you were seeing something you ought not?"

"I sensed it."

"How did you sense it?"

"By the shame and embarrassment I felt."

"When she finally saw you, did she scold and threaten you?"

"Why should she scold and threaten me, Alexis? *I* had done nothing wrong. The door was not even shut. But then, I suspect that you are implying human parents often shift the blame to the offspring, as when they punish out of anger. They say, 'That child makes me furious. If he did not make me furious, I would not have to beat him.' "

"That is the general idea," he said. "But what did she say to you? Did she make excuses? Did she tell you not to tattle?"

I looked again at the clean innocence of the room. "No,"

I said. "I had the feeling she would have liked me to tattle. It had something to do with the spite. She only smiled and said, 'What is it, Willful?' I felt quite foolish, modesty prickling all over me, and said, 'I forgot.' "

"And did you tattle on her?"

"No. That is, only to Della — which was not tattling at all."

"And what did Della think about it?"

"Della helped me to come to the temporary conclusion that it was a thing done in place of going to church. For, later on, we saw my father and his lady friends sneaking off to the dark corners of the house, too. And it all came about at the time the church-attending was banned, except through spite."

"Did you have any idea what the Guide Book said about sex, Hellbent?"

"Not at that time. Later I learned that the Guide Book did not frown upon sex at all, providing one kept to the rules."

"Which were?"

"Either be married or behave and, once married, remain faithful."

"Well, now," he said. "That sounds simple enough."

I gave him a long, cold look. "Do not try to trick me, Alexis," I said. "By now, I am on to your arguments. Also, I can cough up a few of *your* sins. I seem to recall that some of *you* looked upon the daughters of men and found them fair and begat giants — "

"Ah, ah, Hellbent!" he warned, waggling a forefinger. "That was 'the sons of God.' "

"Well? Aren't you a 'son of God'?"

He rocked back on his heels and looked at me chidingly. "As far as you are concerned, Hellbent, I am a celestial being sent to minister for you. You cannot know all the mysteries. You must first gain entrance. But then, I am also 'on to you.' You have dragged in this bit of foolishness to divert my attention from the main question, which is: How deeply ingrained

44

in you was the idea that sex was a substitute for religion? Or did you only accept this idea superficially because it gave permission later to your own desires and deeds?"

"If you are trying to trick me into confessing fornication, Alexis, you need not bother. We both know I am guilty. Quite guilty. And I would still not be a bit unhappy if the accumulations of my sins were to condemn me to hell. In the hope of this, I will add another sin to the pile and make excuses for my later behavior. Yes, as a child I was confused by the substitution. As an adolescent, I had figured out the right and the wrong of it but I did not care. I had, in the meantime, been exposed to more denominational harangues and had concluded that if the prize for behaving according to the Guide Book were to be an eternity spent with such wretches, then I would as soon aim for the opposite."

"Would you like to explain the harangues, Hellbent?"

"Gladly. Realizing that Della and I had in all probability seen and heard too much, both sets of relatives set out to rectify the injury by inflicting two other injuries. My mother's relatives taught us that sex and the body were bad and vulgar. My father's relatives taught us that there was nothing any more wrong with sex and the body than with eating, sleeping, drinking, smoking or any other physical pleasure."

"Kettles of pottage," said Alexis. "How could two such opposites come from such simple rules? And what were the conclusions?"

I grunted. "The first concluded, somehow, that He loved babies but could not tolerate His Own design for procreating them. The second concluded that 'moderation' was the key unlatching the door to all forgiveness. They were especially vague as to whether the 'moderation' should occur inside or outside marriage since, of course, my father was one of their flock and equally guilty with my mother."

"And you decided, from this muddle, that it would be more pleasant all around for you to permit their belief to send

45

them in the one direction while you determinedly aimed for the other?"

"Yes. But I have another excuse for my later wickedness, too, Alexis. Actually, this had more to do with Him than I knew at the time. You see, I had come to the knowledge, by the time I had come to the sin, that there is within each of us a curiously insatiable longing for *something* not given us in the everyday fulfilment of hungers. That is, in eating, sleeping, merry-making. I deluded myself for a time into thinking sex was the satisfaction of this longing. But that was years and years later."

We had left the bedroom and walked down the long hallway to the two flights of stairs. Alexis sidestepped a small dog, which turned and stared after him for a moment with its head tilted. Two little boys ran up the steps and through me on their way to the bathroom. And then we passed through the kitchen and out to the back porch.

"I am glad I am what I am," Alexis mused, sniffing the warm air. "Nor do I especially look forward to the time when your species takes up the task of judging ours. But then I assume that there are many mysteries which shall be made clear to me, too. Shall we walk for a spell, Hellbent? Would you rather I called you Willful?"

"Hellbent is fine," I said. "Keep it that way. When I have finished elaborating the contradictions in which I have been saturated, you will agree with me."

Alexis elevated his brows, but he did not comment. We walked across the green lawn and out to the road.

CHAPTER 9

WE CAME PRESENTLY TO THE RED brick schoolhouse and Alexis stopped to look at it. "Is this where you attended, Hellbent?"

"Yes. Though I was not much of a student."

"Oh? I thought you were a rather good student?"

"As far as marks were concerned, yes. But I was really not much interested. There was no one to impress, save Della, who loved me as I was. And I had come to resent rules in any form."

"Did you know what the Guide Book says of obedience to magistrates?"

"Oh, yes. I only said I resented rules, not that I broke them."

"You mean *at this time*. For I believe we have established that you did break a few — "

"All right, all right," I said sourly. "You don't have to rub it in. I mean 'at this time.' Also, I had rules made by society in mind, and keeping to those is at least more than I can say for my cousins, who broke the laws that were man-made, religion-made, and those extracted from the Guide Book, both written and implied."

"Dear, dear," he said. "But then, since we have come down here so that you could plead your case, let's be on with it. What sort of shenanigans did they pull?"

47

"All the obvious ones. The ones you would expect non-Believers to pull. They skipped school, cheated on exams, lied, gossiped, bullied, listened to and used foul language, cheated in games and sports, fought, argued, molested — "

"I say, Hellbent," Alexis interrupted, "this is rather petty stuff."

"Not so petty, Alexis, when you claim to be a member of an organization of Example-Setters. You must admit that any organization which, on the one hand, imposes such a mountain of rules and regulations as to make membership nearly unbearable and then, on the other hand, runs about wildly evangelizing and encouraging proselytes is of itself bewildering enough without the added complexity of breaking not only its own but everyone else's laws."

Alexis sighed. "I see what you mean," he said. "But then, we were talking about *young* people . . ."

"Young people, indeed," I snorted. "Have you ever seen a bad habit get better with age? Great oaks from little acorns, remember? But I'll get to the adults later. To go on with the young people, one of the cruelest and most effective of their deadly weapons was that of snobbery. They formed little cliques which, for one reason or another, excluded all other young people. The bases for these cliques were generally ridiculous. With boys, for instance, a clique might be composed of those who were related by blood or marriage, those who sang well together, those who played instruments well together, those of approximately the same height, those who had scored the winning points in a game, those who had shared in some tidbit of mischief and so on ad infinitum.

"With the girls, the cloisters were founded even more absurdly. The color of one's hair might be the determining factor, or the style, or the similarity of apparel or size, or lack of beauty or intelligence, or overabundance of either or both, and this, too, ad nauseam. Thus if any other young person, who differed ever so slightly, sought entry into the clique, he was utterly ignored at the least. And if he or she insisted upon entry by being so bold as to sit down next to you and smile, then the only thing left to do was to get up and move away. The mentally retarded and the poverty stricken might as well stay home to begin with, for if those whose mannerisms and appearance varied a shade were let out, then how could the extreme case hope for approval? And all this, mind you, from Believers whose Founder said, 'All ye are brethren,' and Who ministered to the poor, the lonely, the unwanted, the diseased, the blind, the crippled, the demon-possessed!"

"Yes," Alexis said sadly. "To get right down to bare facts, He was even buried in a borrowed grave. But then, you must not forget, Hellbent, that the very fact that they are Believers makes them prey for the Enemy. Satan, the blighter, doesn't have to molest his own. He seeks to corrupt those who are not his own. Much of this behavior sounds as if he had a hand in it."

"Much of it also *looked*," I grunted, "as if they gave him control quite willingly! I recall the incident of the tractor-driving, for example."

"Tractor-driving? One of those farm vehicles?"

"Exactly. Some of my cousins were farmers, you see, and according to state law were not then permitted to procure a license to drive an automobile until they had attained the age of sixteen. However, no license was required to operate farm machinery. Their fathers, therefore, (who were pillars of the church) allowed them, from the time they were able, by stretching, to reach the various apparatuses, to drive the tractors not only all over the countryside but through the village streets at a breakneck speed. Now I think you will agree, Alexis, that despite the fact no civil law was broken, surely a moral law was greatly violated, and that He is surely the Sole Implanter of the moral law into our minds. One cannot heedlessly endanger others without breaking the moral law."

Alexis shook his head. "But I would have thought the state should correct *its* laws!"

"Oh, the police spoke to the fathers now and again and

49

asked that they discipline the youngsters. But why foist personal responsibility off on the state? Besides, this is just one small example of sidestepping civil law. I seem to recall many Believers in the early churches (though I ran across few in the organizations I visited in my lifetime, because they would have been unwelcome, I am sure) were brought forth from the ranks of the criminal, immoral and dishonorable. I also seem to recall that they did not remain in those conditions long. In fact, the whole gist of the conversion, as far as I can see, was '. . . that ye have put off the old man with his deeds and have put on the new man.' I saw no such change, nor anything closely resembling it."

"I can see how you would be disillusioned, Hellbent," Alexis said, starting to walk down the maple-lined street, carefully avoiding the cracks in the sidewalk. "However, the Believer does have two foes to combat. His fleshly nature and his spiritual nature. By spiritual *nature*, I refer to that inner self which delights in sins of the spirit: feeling superiority, embarrassing others, gossiping, shifting blame to the innocent. This is the foe with which the Devil, may he dwell in a crematory, likes most to tamper with because these sins are worse than, and often trigger, those of the flesh. After all, he is the prince of this world, and Believers are dwelling in territory occupied by him."

"It's no use your defending them and making excuses for them, Alexis," I said, watching his footwork. "If they really wanted to change, they would be given the strength to stop throwing in with him and making his work easier. The Guide Book says so. There! You've missed one! You've stepped on a crack!"

Alexis laughed and began to walk straight. "So I have," he said, "so I have. But then, we're just nicely started. I'll have another go at it later." He seemed rather disgustingly amused.

CHAPTER 10

TWO BLOCKS DOWN THE STREET we turned left. A streak of sunlight splashed between the round polka-dot shadows and, for a moment, caught Alexis in its embrace. He glinted brilliantly, until I was quite blinded for a second or two, but then we passed on into the shade again and shortly I was able to focus.

We came then to a large cream-colored building set close to the sidewalk, and Alexis stopped to look up at the steeple.

"Would you like to tell me about it?" he asked.

"I wish I had a body," I said. "I would like to shudder. This, as you already know Alexis, is the church of my mother's relatives. I cannot tell you how many times — "

But suddenly a car drew up at the curb, a door opened, and to my complete horror out stepped Aunt Fussy. I let out a yelp and jumped behind Alexis. Aunt Fussy gathered up the Dutch oven from the front seat and hissed at the driver, "See you're here to pick me up at two sharp, Grim. I don't mean to get stuck with all the dishes from this luncheon! You just be here and act insistent on my coming home, hear?" Uncle Grim nodded like a perpetual-motion bird and drove off. Aunt Fussy bustled on into the building, pot in hand, and gave the door a kick behind her.

"You can come out now," Alexis said. "Have I not made it clear enough to you that they are unable to see you, Hellbent? And why all the demonstration over a harmless old lady?"

"Harmless old lady!" I shrieked. "She's a witch! Did you miss the stoop to Uncle Grim's shoulders? (Though I admit he's a good match for her.) Did you hear the way she plots to shift the work to others and exonerate herself? She's been manipulating and bossing, setting others in the wrong in order to elevate herself all of her life! Under the cloak of pretended sweetness, she attempts to govern the lives of everyone she comes near. With a coo and a sigh of concern she suggests whom they should marry, how they should dress, what they should cook, how many children they should have, how they should keep them healthy — and why do you just stand there staring at me? Didn't you just finish saying that the sins of the spirit are the worst kind? I cannot begin to tell you the number of times this squawking guinea hen has pulled Della and me by the ears to this or that potluck, forcing all manner of questionable concoctions — Alexis, what *are* you staring at?"

But then I knew. Directly through me passed Cousin Prissy! "Oh, no!" I moaned. "Alexis, let us please get out of this place. Before you know it, the whole tribe — "

"Relax, Hellbent. They can't see you, hear you, touch you or even smell you. You are in a suspended state. You have left your physical matter and have not yet assumed true spiritual matter. So go on with the potluck. Like most children, I take it, you and Della did not enjoy suspicious-looking food?"

"Indeed we did not! Della would whisper, wrinkling her nose at each casserole she was made to try, 'I wish I had a hot-dog.' (For in those days, with our parents living lewdly and loudly, hot-dogs were our mainstay.) But of course all this wish got her was a sound kick in the shin beneath the table."

Alexis chuckled. "Sounds normal," he said.

"Normal!" I roared. "Then I would say that normality

52

needs a good revision! To kick a child for honesty? To try to pass dishonesty off as 'good manners'? Besides, you should have heard Aunt Fussy once *she* was out of earshot. She would pucker and sniff and say, 'Grim, don't you agree that pie crust was tough as corrugated cardboard? And that rice was cooked to the consistency of laundry starch, to be sure. And the gravy was thickened brine . . .' And Uncle Grim would shake his head dolefully and whine, 'We must not expect happiness in this world, Fussy. Only in the next, only in the next, only in the next. We must bear the burden of today and look to tomorrow . . .' (His remarks were always irrelevant, so Aunt Fussy always took them to mean whatever she wished.) 'You are quite right, Grim,' she would say. 'The thing for me to do is to be charitable. In the morning I shall call each of those ladies and give her *my* recipe — the one the church has used these many years . . .' "

Alexis shook his head. "You are beginning to make more sense," he admitted. "Go on."

"Well, Alexis, if I have given you the impression that our relatives bickered with and maligned their Shepherds and the Believers of other churches, this was mere groundwork for what went on among themselves. In the matter of food, for instance, Aunt Fussy and her cohorts had a perpetual competition going as to which of them should swoop down upon younger, or newer, lady members and hand out the denominational recipes. 'So that,' Aunt Fussy would purr, 'all the barbecue will taste alike, dear.' What she really meant was: 'So that *yours* will not taste better than *mine*.' And of course the same held true of gelatin salads, Christmas cookies, tuna casseroles and, most of all, denominational chili. In fact, that was what she had in the pot she just carried in."

"Denominational chili?" Alexis said, scowling.

"Right," I said. "That was Aunt Fussy's idea of what the Mexicans should have stewed together had they had the good sense to consult her. And to deviate from her recipe was to sin. The times I have heard brides (married in from other

53

churches) verbally trounced for being so innocent as to use the original formula are countless. Aunt Fussy would taste the mixture, wince, and then say delicately, 'My dear, did you use chili beans, instead of kidney? Tomato sauce, instead of whole, canned tomatoes? Braised beef, instead of hamburger?' And if the young thing confessed that she had, Aunt Fussy would draw a deep breath and pronounce grandly, 'I will see you get my recipe, child — the recipe used in *this* church — before you are asked to work on another committee . . .'"

Alexis nodded. "I can see there is some spiritual sin involved," he said grudgingly. "However, that is not unforgivable."

"Of course not," I grunted. "Which is my whole point."

He gave me a long look. "Before we get into that again, see if I have the names of these brews correct? Barbecue? Chili? Tuna casserole? I should like to taste them. Do you suppose if we went inside —"

"But I thought it was not necessary for you to eat?"

He shook his head. "Not *necessary*. But completely *possible*. Have you forgotten the two angels Lot entertained? They ate unleavened bread."

"But they had taken on the total form of men. You have a man's form visible to me, but no substance."

But before he could answer, another car pulled to the curb. I groaned. "Cousin Bumptious," I explained. "He was one of the tractor-driving bunch. He's letting off Aunt Priggish. She's a widow now. Uncle Heedless passed upward three years ago. Probably worked his way around several rules by now . . ."

"Don't be here before two-thirty," Aunt Priggish was saying sharply to Cousin Bumptious. "Fussy and that finicky daughter of hers will want to get out of the dishwater as soon as Grim shows up to make excuses for them, so *I* will have to stay here and see the kitchen's cleaned up proper!" But Bumptious was already down the street and rounding the corner on two wheels. Aunt Priggish closed her mouth to a tight line and marched in to take command.

Alexis blinked after her and said softly, "Pellets of hail . . . But then, Hellbent, to get back to your question, do not be too fooled by substance and matter. You have just removed yourself from the throes of the atomic age wherein it was proven possible to transmute concrete to ephemeral haze. Spirituality, therefore, being indestructible, may prove to be more substantial than matter as you know it. At least do not continue to frustrate your actions, or mine, with schoolboy science involving weights, measurements and density. Shall we go in and see what they are about?"

"All right," I sighed. "If you insist."

CHAPTER 11

THE INSIDE OF THE CHURCH was dim and deserted except for the chattering of the women and the clanging of pots and pans in the kitchen. Alexis paused to look around the auditorium, from its carpeted aisles and tufted pews to the top of the single stained glass window and the scattered paintings around it. Here, he shook his head and drew up the corner of his mouth. "Raphael certainly left his mark, didn't he? Honestly, Hellbent, do I look even remotely like a nude overweight infant?"

I glanced from Alexis to the pink winged babies and back again. "These never used to be here," I said. "And, no, you don't. But you might if you chose, or were so assigned, I imagine."

"'Imagine!'" he grunted, walking slowly on. "There is a thing you creatures do a great deal of. And therein lies the basis of most of your problems."

"Also most of our progress," I suggested. "Can you imagine how far we should have got without imagination?"

"Progress!" he snorted. "You call it progress when, after numerous years of delving and experimenting, you finally come upon a scrap of knowledge or a tinkering bit of machinery *He* knew about from the beginning? I wonder that you dare use the reason He gave you to reason against Him." And he shook his head.

"I would agree with that," I said. "But I would also contend that each of us is required to use to the utmost the abilities given him. We cannot simply sit here and say, 'He already knows and can do everything, so why try?' Nor will you argue, surely, that each will be held responsible for what he did or did not accomplish with what he was given."

Alexis stopped at the door to the dining room and looked at me. "That," he said, "from one who cannot forgive his own relatives their little personality quirks?"

"I never said I couldn't forgive them, Alexis. I have only made quite plain that I can't tolerate living with them. However, if it would excuse me from their eternal presence, I would even lie and say I have not forgiven them. But please let us get on with your food sampling so that we may be out of this place."

The dining room was set up for the luncheon. Three long tables were set end to end and covered with white paper. The dishes were set in proper style with paper napkins on each plate.

"Well," said Alexis, glancing about, "this is less decorous than *I* would have imagined . . ."

I looked at him curiously, but he made no signs of elaborating.

We stood then at the kitchen doorway and watched the women bustling about, talking as they stirred this and seasoned that.

"I hope that mortician remembers to bring some of the flowers back," said Aunt Priggish, giving the spoon handle a crack against the side of the pot. "Can't count on anyone to get anything done proper these days. Fussy, are you sure you remembered to tell him?"

Aunt Fussy sent her an impatient glance and hunched her shoulders. "Of course, Prig. After all, it was *my* idea to use the funeral flowers for center pieces to begin with, wasn't it? Put in enough time and effort on that one when he was alive,

57

we have. Poor Grim and I trotted the little heathen off to church and preached the right way to him and Della — "

I gasped aloud and Alexis burst out laughing. "*Me?*" I choked. "Are they talking about *me?* This is the luncheon planned to take place after *my* funeral? I am at this moment being *inhumed?*"

Alexis could not seem to stop laughing. " 'O death, where is thy sting'?" he chortled. " 'O grave, where is thy victory'?"

"Sting, indeed!" I snapped. "Don't forget I still have to spend enternity with these sorcerers! Look at them. *Look* at them! Serving that potion after *my* funeral!"

"Maybe," said Cousin Prissy then, "we should have used linen napkins . . ."

"Nonsense!" said Aunt Fussy. "That would be just too much work for nothing."

"Hmmph!" said Aunt Priggish. "*I* should have been the one to wash them. I think, Fussy, if you would change bleaches — "

"And cause thread-breaks in all my fine linens? I should think not! Besides, who in Hellbent history ever knew *her* side of the family to do a thing right? They won't even notice."

"You are probably right about that," Aunt Priggish agreed. "Has anyone heard where she is? Last I heard Chaser had thrown her over and she was scrubbing floors in some tavern until such time as she could draw a pension. Poor Taunt. Never should have married that tramp. Tried to tell him."

"Maybe," said Cousin Prissy, "we should have used soup spoons . . ."

"Nonsense!" said Aunt Fussy. "They would only shovel more down them if we did. I should like a little dab to take home for Grim. Has one of those miserable summer colds, you know. I told him not even to attempt going to the funeral. There are Cousins enough to carry the casket, and not much of anyone will be there, anyway, except snoopers, considering the way he died . . ."

"Good idea," said Aunt Priggish. "That's one less pot *I*

shall have to scrub. Anyone heard whether Taunt is out of the sanitarium as yet? Probably not. Too bad he never found a woman of his own belief . . . Shouldn't have drunk like that if he had . . ."

Alexis was scowling now. "I must admit that I am confused, Hellbent. Did you not say this is the church of your *mother's* relatives?"

"Yes," I whispered, though it wasn't necessary. "That is, when my mother was still married to my father. But I explained to you that when they broke up, their relatives somehow did an about-face and joined the other's church. These are my father's relatives, you see, working in what used to be my mother's church. The ones they are cooking for, and expecting after the funeral, will be my mother's relatives, who now attend what used to be my father's church." Then I added with a snicker, "This is going to be more fun than I thought."

Alexis raised his brows, and we resumed eavesdropping.

"I shall be glad to see their faces when they see the new carpeting," Aunt Fussy said. "They did very little to keep the place up as we have. In fact, I don't mind admitting that I feel quite proud of my charity, offering to have the luncheon here before *they* got a chance to have it *there*. I understand that place is a shambles since we withdrew . . ."

"Especially," said Aunt Priggish, "since you knew you could count on me for seventy-five per cent of the work and seeing things were done proper. Are you sure you remembered the mortician?"

Aunt Fussy wriggled all over. "Honestly, Prig!"

"Maybe," said Cousin Prissy, "we should have bought oyster crackers . . ."

"Nonsense!" said Aunt Fussy. "Let them grind the things up in their fists if they must have them in their bowls. And if you don't stop finicking over every little detail, I shall send you back to work. No use your taking the afternoon off if it is to make a wreck of you. Poor girl," she said then to Aunt Priggish. "Been a bundle of nerves ever since she broke up

59

with Shrewd Strategy. I keep telling her that if the man cannot see things our way, the *right* way, then she's better off — "

But Cousin Prissy put her hands to her face and ran sobbing from the room. Aunt Fussy would have rattled on about the affair, but the front door of the building opened and the mortician's assistant arrived with the flowers. The others came along behind, so there was no time for personal elaboration.

"While they are all out greeting one another," Alexis said, tiptoeing toward the stove, "I shall taste the chili."

"Alexis!" I warned. "Be careful — "

But it was too late. He had ladled a portion directly into his mouth. In the next instant the spoon clattered to the floor, Alexis clutched his throat, and I went for the water tap. Unfortunately, I could not turn it on, having no hands.

"Lumps of Lucifer!" Alexis gasped. "I have tasted hell!"

To which I could not help laughing, "My precise opinion for forty years!"

CHAPTER 12

WHILE ALEXIS WAS RECOVERING himself and vowing hereafter to abide by the knowledge he had been given and not tamper with what was not intended to be his concern, I stood by the kitchen doorway and watched the relatives trickle in and knot together greeting each other. Their smiles were wooden. Their remarks razor-edged.

"Come," I said, motioning Alexis away from the sink. "I'll point them out to you."

"Stop gesturing," he said. "When will you remember that you only stir the air?"

But I forfeited the pleasure of answering him for the better game of listening to relatives. "That's Uncle Stern," I said, when Alexis was at my side. "And that's Uncle Harsh. And that's Aunt Sedate. And there's Cousin Blowzy. And there's Uncle Lofty. And Aunt Severe. And Cousin Strict. Cousin Strict is the son of Aunt Severe and Uncle Stern. Cousin Blowzy is Cousin Bump's brother. Aunt Sedate is married to Uncle Lofty. Uncle Harsh is a widower . . ."

"I don't see Della," Alexis said.

"You won't," I promised. "She wouldn't be caught dead with this pack. Or, perhaps," I snickered, "that's the only way she *would* be caught! But listen. They speak for themselves."

"Did you notice the new carpeting?" Aunt Fussy said,

extending a hand to Aunt Sedate. "Looks much better than it did, wouldn't you say?"

"I noticed," said Aunt Sedate, gathering herself up. "If you are the sort concerned with material possessions, I can see how it would be impressive."

"Mmm," said Aunt Fussy. "The stained glass window has been repaired, too. And some paintings added. Did you see?"

Aunt Sedate looked straight forward. "We have painted the inside of our auditorium dead white and have removed that musty cushioning and varnished the pews — "

"Well!" said Aunt Fussy. "If you feel that does honor to *Him* . . ."

Aunt Sedate's expression was unchanging. "We believe He was a Plain Man, meek and lowly."

"Lowly!" said Cousin Blowzy, joining the pair. "How lowly could a King get? Myself, I take it He was a bit of a connoisseur. Knew a good thing when He saw it and didn't mind speaking His tongue. Say, isn't that stuff cooked yet? Gives a man an appetite standing out in the graveyard listening to a bunch of lies about old Willy."

"Of all the *nerve!*" I spat. But Alexis waved me silent as another batch of them arrived. "Who are these?" he asked.

I bypassed my exasperation and grunted, "That's Uncle Crafty and Aunt Sparing. They're from my mother's side. And that's Cousin Trifle, from my father's side. And Cousin Timorous, from my mother's side. Uncle Stoic and Aunt Stolid, from my mother's side. Cousin Rational, Cousin Staid and Cousin Obstinate, from my father's side. Cousin Flounder, Cousin Hasty and Cousin Fancy . . ."

"Enough," said Alexis. "I shall figure the rest out. They are about to sit down. I want to hear them pray."

They gathered around the tables and a moment of silence and throat-clearing followed. "Harsh," said Aunt Fussy, taking charge as always, "since you are the eldest, would you — ?"

Uncle Harsh, at the end of the table, scraped his chair loudly as he arose. "Our God and our Father," he chanted nasally, "we have come together to mourn one who has submitted to sin and violence . . ."

He paused for the amens, while I shouted, "Hogwash!" and Alexis shooshed and motioned to me. "Maintain yourself, Hellbent!"

"We have no doubt but that his soul shall writhe in torment," Uncle Harsh went on. "Therefore, let those of us remaining take heed of ourselves and keep to Thy ways, as we understand them, and learn from the horrible example set before us. For we know that Thou art a God of Terrible Punishment and hast laid down laws which must be kept. We stand before You with a free conscience, knowing each of us has, in his own small way, done his best to assist the infidel passed from our midst. We ask no leniency, for Thou art Unbending. Only apply this lesson to our lives and keep it before us as a reminder of what we must be and do. For we ask it all in His Name . . ."

"That monster!" I ground out. "That vile, despicable, loathesome, detestable, odious, heinous, repulsive — "

"Hellbent," Alexis warned, "if you are not soon silent, I will request Divine Power to halt your permission to speak at all! Now, I have been sent down here on a mission, on *your* behalf, so do try to contain yourself and allow me to determine how well-founded your complaints are and what should be done about them. If you had only remained quiet, this *might* have been a score for your side. Up to now you have aired mostly sniveling little gripes but not a lot of actual malpractice. If you sincerely want to win your case, stop giving in to these juvenile displays."

He looked as if he meant business — as if he might fan his fingers before my face and say, "Poof!" and I would be silenced.

"Sorry," I murmured. "Not another word."

They began to eat then, and Alexis walked slowly around the table, motioning me to follow at his heels, and listened to scraps of conversation.

63

"Have you heard from Vex lately?" Aunt Priggish asked Aunt Sparing. "I heard she was – uh – working in some sort of establishment . . ."

"We haven't heard *directly* from her since she left," said Aunt Sparing. "No one has. Not even Della. But friends of some friends of ours said that someone *sounding* like her had bought part interest in a – uh – *restaurant*. You see, I understand she got quite a settlement from Thrill when they parted . . . Our side of the family was always quite – *watchful* about money . . ."

"Speaking of money," Cousin Blowzy chimed in, "how'd you come out with that lawsuit, Uncle Crafty? Take the township for a good haul, did you?"

Uncle Crafty's eyes narrowed. "No need for humor, Blowzy," he said coldly. "As I see it, business is business and *He* would be the last to be wasteful or negligent. I remember He stretched a few loaves a long way and picked up the fragments."

"Makes good sense to me," said Cousin Rational. "Can't let people make fools of us."

"I agree to that," said Uncle Stern. "Trouble with Believers is that we give the impression we're too soft. Got to let them know we aren't pushovers. Look at what *He* did to the moneychangers in the temple. Can't stand for any nonsense."

"Getting back to money," Blowzy broke in, "I suppose old Willy left everything to Della and that adopted daughter of hers?"

Several snickers rippled around the table.

"Adopted indeed," said Cousin Fancy, brushing crumbs from her ruffled blouse. "Whatever reputation the rest of us had left was blown to bits by that little maneuver."

"See what I mean?" said Aunt Fussy to Cousin Prissy, who had joined the group red-eyed and a few minutes late. "See what comes of getting involved where we oughtn't?"

Cousin Prissy started to cry anew and left the table. Aunt

Fussy shook her head. "Grim and I have done all in our power to protect that girl and here she is, thirty-five, and still so naive . . ."

"That's one thing," said Aunt Severe, "that I was glad to note Harsh mentioned in his prayer. Each of *us* has done his best or her best to set an example. If Vex and Taunt went wrong, it was certainly through no weakness on our part. If I said it once, I said it a hundred times, 'Stern, we have done our level best. If those two refuse to shape up, then they will have to face the consequences.'"

Cousin Timorous shivered. "I'm afraid of *Him*," she said. "When I think of all He can do — and all He did to the Israelites . . ."

"Mustn't get emotional," said Aunt Stolid. "Do what's right and you have no need to get wrought up in the one direction or the other."

"As far as I can seem to make out," Uncle Stoic added, "that was their whole problem: too concerned with pleasure and pain. Wanted the pleasure for themselves and the pain for the other fellow. That's no fit or healthy outlook."

"I can't see what difference it makes," said Cousin Trifle with a shrug. "What's done is done, and He'll get His way anyway, so why worry? The thing is, to go on. Does Vicie know that Cousin Willful is her real father and that Della only adopted her to get him off the hook?"

There were a couple of gasps, but Blowzy laughed out loud.

"Well," said Cousin Fancy, "everyone in our set has whispered it, so it's just as well somebody shouted it. I've done my best to keep up appearances, but it hasn't been easy. The only compensating thought I have is that *He* knows what we suffer, and *He* will reward . . ."

Cousin Strict nodded. "That's a good point, Fancy. It's a pity none of us could get that across to Willful while there was still hope. Poor damned soul. If he'd only let us get within speaking distance, we might have changed his entire course — "

"I'm with Trifle," said Cousin Obstinate. "What's done is done. Willful had his chance and he blew it. No sense mourning over the past and no sense wishing *He* would change the rules. Willful's got his just desserts."

"Speaking of desserts," said Blowzy, "didn't you say something about apple squares, Mumsy?"

Aunt Priggish fluttered and pretended annoyance. "Naughty boy," she chided, and hurried off to the kitchen.

For a moment there was silence and then Cousin Rational said, "That was some preposterous performance old Della put on at graveside this morning, pretending to faint and having to be carried off."

"It scared me," said Cousin Timorous. "I thought she'd tip over the casket and I thought, 'What if he came rolling out . . .'"

"Nothing to get excited about," said Cousin Staid. "Just Della's way of getting out of doing the decent thing, coming to the luncheon with the rest of us. Never took a responsibility seriously in her whole life. Never took *Him* seriously, either, or she'd have mended her ways. What was the frivolous idea of having that Doctor from the Theological Seminary preach the sermon, anyway? Even if she bore a childish grudge against the old Shepherds, she could have asked the new ones. But that's Della. Flighty even at a time like this."

Cousin Flounder shifted in his chair. "You know, I was wondering about that myself. Spoke in such concepts that I didn't understand a word he said. Did any of the rest of you? I have a hard enough time getting things straight as it is, without some high-sounding professor fouling me up."

"That was undoubtedly the idea," said Uncle Lofty. "Della's way of striking out at us and, at the same time, consoling herself. The context of the eulogy, which she hoped would be above our heads, was that Willful understood more about *Him* than we suspected and, whether or not we liked it, he was as deserving as any of the rest of us. Those big words don't tangle me up, but neither do His teachings. And I can tell you here and now, Della has got another think coming."

There was an interval of head-shaking and tongue-clicking and then Cousin Hasty rose and said, "Well, I must be off. I'm chairman of a little study group which meets at two. Have a three-thirty appointment with the music director about the new choir robes. At four, I meet with the quartet. Five-fifteen, another rehearsal with the teen-agers. If this hadn't been my day off, I never could have made it at all. Must be about My Father's business, you know . . ."

Shortly thereafter, the luncheon broke up.

CHAPTER 13

WE CAME OUT OF THE CHURCH in time to see Uncle Grim toddle, like an ancient apteryx, up the front walk, glancing at his watch and mumbling to himself. Alexis smiled.

For several minutes we walked in silence. Finally I asked, "Am I off probation?"

He turned to me and nodded, flecks of glitter sprinkling from his head as the sunlight caught the motion. "You are," he said cheerfully. "Erupt to your heart's content."

"I had no intention of erupting!" I said impatiently. "I was going to ask what *you* thought of them — *including* Uncle Harsh's prayer. If that wasn't a clear case of judging — in fact, diabolically wishing to heap coals on my head —"

"I admit," said Alexis, "there's room for improvement."

"Improvement!" I roared. "Can't you see what each one of them is doing? Oh, they believe in *Him*, all right! But then they promptly set about creating images in their own likeness, mongrel gods cross bred between misapplied excerpts from the Guide Book and projections of their own characteristics! Mind you, I don't say *qualities*, because the very word itself implies some good, and the characteristics which dominate most of them and which they seem, for some adverse reason, to want to find excuse for and to worship are not even remotely akin to 'good.' Take Uncle Crafty always wanting to beat somebody out, for instance. Cousin Fancy always putting the emphasis on 'position.' Cousin Hasty spreading himself so thin he only half does everything. You see what I mean, Alexis? They are like artists who paint self-portraits and then set them on the shelf and stand back and say, 'You are my god!' You see?"

"I see very well, Hellbent," he said mildly. "And I agree that it would have taken a great deal of patience to get along with them."

"Patience," I snorted. "Patience indeed! Why are they so stubborn? Why do they *insist* upon remaining blind to their own narrow outlooks and blundering ways? Don't they honestly know that they hurt people? Or is it that they don't care? I'll make a confession to you, Alexis. An honest and sincere confession. There is nothing more painful than to see a truth objectively and remain incapable of causing others to see it. That is worse than any hell I can imagine."

Alexis stopped walking and turned to look at me. For a moment that was all he did. Just look at me. Finally he said, "Is that a park behind me, where I heard children laughing a moment ago?"

"Yes," I said, looking beyond his shoulder. "Sort of. It's a playground. They are playing tag. They have run around to the other side now."

He nodded. "Let us go over there and sit for a while. Children play with an innocent abandon. It reminds me of Home."

We crossed the street to the playground and sat on a green bench and watched half a dozen youngsters romp over the velvet grass, up to the slide, under the swings and across to the parallel bars that were "it."

After a while Alexis said quietly, "You were telling me your reason for committing suicide, I believe."

I turned and stared at him. "I was no such thing!"

"Ah, but you were, Hellbent. You had just said that it was worse than any hell you could imagine to recognize a truth and be unable to get others to see it. Much less *do* something about it. I think that was what you were implying."

I stared at him a moment longer and finally said, "All right. If you must know the truth (and of course you already do), the beginning of Uncle Harsh's prayer angered me even more than the last of it, his ruinous and sanctimonious judgment. That bit about 'one who has *submitted* to sin and violence.' In order to submit, one must have been pursued. I was never 'pursued' by sin, Alexis, except as it was personified by my parents' relatives! Violence did not 'pursue' me, nor did I 'submit' to it. On the contrary, *I* was the pursuer, and I *invited* the sin and violence! There. Is that what you wanted me to say? That I deliberately and willfully committed suicide in the hope that such monstrous transgression would absolve His promise to me as a Believer? In other words, hoping the act of violence would free me to go to hell?"

Alexis turned to me and smiled. *Smiled!*

"Alexis," I snapped, "did you hear me at all?"

"Of course," he said. "I was just thinking how infantile your little rebellion was. Rather like a three-year-old who packs up to leave home because he does not like his brothers and sisters."

I felt some of the starch go out of me. "If you are implying that I didn't get far, you are of course quite right."

"Well," he said consolingly, "the parents would not let the three-year-old get far, either."

I got up impatiently. "I was not a three-year-old," I said. "I was forty! And I was sick to death — literally to *death* — of Believers purporting to be one thing and behaving like quite another, ebbing farther away from Reality. He *is* the only Real Thing, you know . . ."

Alexis smiled gently. "But you were willing to give all that up? Consummation more glorious than anything you could begin to imagine? For you had only come to the outer outskirts, Hellbent. You had not seen anything at all really. You had only the assurance of having arrived. You know infinite happiness lies in store for you if — "

"But how can it?" I bellowed. "The very proof that it

70

cannot lies in the fact that we are *here,* you and I! All this free will! If it is permissible for me, it is permissible for *them!* They will be allowed to go right on blundering and interfering and dictating and thinking they are always right — "

"But it does not work that way, Hellbent — "

"Then how in the world *does* it work?"

"That's just it. It does not work *in the world's* ways at all. But I am not at liberty to tell you any more right now than you have already been told in the Guide Book. It's all there, Hellbent. How can you know so many of the promises and not know them all? How can you accept only part and reject the rest? In a way, you are very like the rest . . ."

"I am not! I accept and adhere to more than *they* do! I know there are mysteries — "

"But you cannot accept complete compatibility as one of the mysteries which will be resolved?"

I moved back and forth. "The children have gone home, Alexis. Shall we move on?"

"Hellbent," he scolded, "you are hedging . . ."

"All right, all right! Maybe if I could *see* — maybe if I could really *know* . . ."

"But that is impossible. The first thing is to trust. If you can believe and accept and have got as far as the outer outskirts, I do not see why you cannot submit completely — "

"That's Earth-logic!" I snorted. "That's like people saying, 'If you can believe the first three verses of Genesis, you can believe everything else in the Guide Book.' And still people doubt some of the rest of It, don't they? The most important parts of It?"

Alexis sighed and got to his feet. "I can see that we are up against a brick wall here. The only way you can know for sure, according to your way of thinking, that the happiness (or compatibility, if you will) is infinite and sublime is to see it for yourself and the only way you can see it for yourself is to trust . . ."

"Oh, sure! And by the time I find out they're all running

around filled with free will, the pearly gate will have clicked shut behind me and there I'll be, stuck with them!"

"Try not to be blasphemous, Hellbent," he said stiffly. "And you were the one, as I recall, who mentioned the fallen angels. There *are* ways out."

"*I* tried one," I reminded.

He smiled forgivingly. "You tried the wrong one, Hellbent. You tried a mere physical revolt . . ."

"But when *I* point out *their* sins of the spirit — "

"Come along, Hellbent," he said, starting to walk away. "I believe this is the street on which Della and her husband first lived? Perhaps you will point out the house to me. I believe you said you went to live with them at the age of seventeen, when Della married . . ."

"Now *you* are hedging!" I accused, following along after him.

"Quite right," he said, not pausing to glance at me. "You see, I hoped we might have gotten to the crux of the thing, what with your seeing all of the relatives together like that. But I realize now we shall probably have to go the whole way. So let us get back to the time of the whole smashup and disintegration of family life. You said your mother moved off with Thrill Chaser, and your father — "

"Married a woman named Ill Fame. My mother moved south. My father moved west."

"And you never saw them again."

"No. I doubt that any of the relatives have, either. Probably all hearsay. None of them are really interested in any of the others, except to dominate."

"And you? Have you never wondered?"

"At first I was too angry and relieved. Later, I wouldn't have known where to start."

"Did you wonder why they never came to you?"

"Sometimes. But if they could leave me in the first place, why should they be inclined to return?"

"People change."

"Not the Hellbents! No, Alexis, it was simply a bad mistake all around. Better forgotten."

"But can you forget? Really?"

I shrugged, lightly swishing the air. "They could apparently. So we tried. Della and I. Non Regenerate helped, I can tell you. There. There's the house. It looks deserted. Shall we go in?"

CHAPTER 14

THE HOUSE WAS A SMALL BUNGALOW at the idle edge of town, away from the highway. It stood apart, the yard overgrown with weeds, the windows naked, the outside in need of painting.

"The village grew in the other direction," I said. "I remember how neat and beautiful this place seemed to Della and me in comparison to the ramshackle way we had lived, toward the last, at home. Non Regenerate bought the place for Della. He was eight years older, you see, and alone, and already set up in his own business. He was a haven."

"And did Della love him?" Alexis asked.

"Of course! Everyone loved him! Except our parents' relatives. They disliked him intensely because he renounced their claim to Della and me and ordered them to cease interfering and, plainly, to leave us alone. 'All that is finished,' he told us. 'Finally and irrevocably over. Forget that phase of your lives. Forget it ever happened. We'll start anew, the three of us, on a foundation built of love without defect.'"

Alexis glanced at me. "By 'defect,'" he said, "he meant religion?"

"Yes. He meant that."

"But religion, in one form or another, is that silver thread tying humans to Him."

"That may well be. But Non Regenerate was more than

ready to snip the thread because of its dual obligation. In fact, because of the dual obligation the thread, for him, had never been properly tied to begin with. That is, *tightly* tied."

"Dual obligation, Hellbent?" Alexis asked.

"Well, Non Regenerate knew of the Guide Book. He knew enough of It to understand that tying one's self to Him meant also tying one's self to his fellow man. Tying one's self to his fellow man meant subjection to fellow man's personal interpretation of Him. In other words, to get involved with Him at all was, to Non Regenerate's way of thinking, to end right up where Della and I had always been. He did not want his life and happiness cluttered so it was simpler to dismiss the whole of it."

"Including Him."

"Yes, Alexis, including Him."

"And you and Della, then. Did your consciences not sting even slightly?"

"Why should they? Hadn't we heard the arguments against conscience-training? If they stung at all, it would only be a matter of reconditioning them to other rules and regulations. Besides, as Della maintained, so much evil had come out of the very goodness that only goodness *could* come out of what our parents' relatives called 'wickedness.' And of course Della's theory proved correct. We were never happier. The self-righteousness, the false mongrel gods, the judging, the snooping, the meddling — all these were in the past. And with them all the sin and vulgarity and shame and humiliation and rage and helplessness."

"But mere branching out into adulthood would dissolve many of these things, Hellbent. Most children, at their parents' hands, feel surges of 'shame and humiliation and rage and helplessness.' Especially at times of punishment."

"You know it wasn't like that with us, Alexis. These feelings in us were not brought about by childhood punishment. They were brought about by adult punishing adult and only inadvertently punishing us."

75

"But if you knew the punishment were not intended for you —"

"We were beyond forgiveness, Alexis. Besides, whom would we have forgiven? Our parents left immediately and to throw in with the relatives meant a continuation of the same old misery. No, there was never any question of forgiveness. Simply a complete finish to the total conflict. Non Regenerate was the key to a whole new concept of living. You see, as far as we could make out, our parents and their relatives had already divorced Him from what they called 'religious life.' So He was, in effect, already out of the picture. All that remained was to remove the bitter pretense of 'living for Him.' It was like putting an end to playing church. It was easily done."

"I see," said Alexis. "And coming here, then, was like coming to a new world, especially after he dispossessed all the relatives and eradicated all tentacles."

"Even more wonderful than coming to a new world. In coming to a new world, one must face hardships, uncertainty, fear. We faced none of those. It was like opening the doors to our hearts and minds and letting the warm, clean sunlight come into every dark, hidden corner. It was like going out on a fresh April morning and drinking in the dewy scent of lilies of the valley. Like watching a rainbow break through the clouds and split the sky wide open after a dismal storm. We stood at the edge of life with the chasm of horror behind us and hand-in-hand, like three orphans starting out on a breath-taking adventure, faced an amber horizon tinged with gold and orange. A new world, Alexis? The very air we breathed tingled with expectancy!"

Alexis nodded solemnly. "Let us go inside," he said.

"Perhaps it's locked . . ."

He turned to me with an indulgent smile. "You are so engrossed in the past that you have forgotten the present, Hellbent." And the next thing I knew we had walked, of course, through the front door and stood in the small, empty parlor.

"But *you* have substance," I said, staring at the whole of him. "Apparently not substance which live people can see, but that little dog — "

His eyes crinkled and his mouth drew up at the corners. "Perhaps it is they who have not the substance then."

"But sometimes we walk through doors, sometimes we go away out around obstacles, sometimes we walk and walk, sometimes we simply *are* . . ."

He sighed heavily. "Do not persist in forgetting our purpose, Hellbent. We are not here to investigate celestial methodology."

He walked about then, looking the place over. "It seems a comfortable dwelling. Small. I should agree it was decent of Non Regenerate to consider you a part of the marriage package."

"It was most decent, Alexis. He even insisted I finish high school and live here for nothing. What little I did earn at part-time work he wanted me to keep for pocket money. He was wonderful to Della, too. 'You are the family I was never fortunate enough to have,' he said. 'I know enough to appreciate you.' He brought us little gifts, he planned outings and surprises, he was interested in everything we thought or said. In fact, he lived closer to Reality, the kind of life I would have thought *He* wanted us to live, than any Believer I ever knew."

"I can see," said Alexis, "where this would be misleading. For Reality to be a mere pretense and for pretense to seem like Reality."

"But there was no 'pretense' in Non Regenerate! He was open and honest and direct! He was completely straightforward and aboveboard!"

Alexis shook his head slowly. "There is deception in all human beings, Hellbent. And especially in those who are aware of the Guide Book and shy away from It. You men-

77

tioned the moral law yourself. You maintained that it was instilled in *each* person *by Him*. As surely as any of your parents' relatives broke this law, so did Non Regenerate. In a more gross way. Rejecting *Him* is the greatest sin of all. According to the Guide Book."

Sadness came upon me and I turned away. "I know," I said slowly. "I know, Alexis."

"And it grieves you to think that he might not live above?"

I shot him a quick look. "It grieves me that *I* might not live below! He was the best friend I ever had! I even used to wish that Della — " But I stopped short.

"That Della?"

"Well, you already know anyway, so I might as well put it into words. I used to wish that Della would bear him a child."

"She refused?"

"Not exactly. She would have tried if he had insisted, but it was not in him to insist on anything which brought unhappiness to others."

"The thought of motherhood made her unhappy?"

"Very. She could not forget our childhood. She tortured herself with thoughts like, 'What if I am only dreaming? What if I were to bear a child and I awoke to find I had a hateful husband and a miserable marriage?' Or, 'What if this is real, but something happened to make it go bad and the child were to suffer? Better not to be born at all . . .' "

"But surely she was not sorry she had been born? Because the first seventeen years were unhappy did not mean that all of life was bad. Especially now that she had gained such freedom."

"I know, Alexis. But she was still a child in many ways. She still had nightmares. She still awoke trembling and weeping. He could not bear for her to suffer. 'Forget about children,' he said. 'We are fine just as we are. Never think about it again.' She relaxed then. She became completely happy."

"She sounds to me more like a child looking for a proper father than a wife who loved her husband."

I glanced at him. "I have heard that in other countries young girls are espoused to older men at an extremely early age. They are taken to the man's house to live. They grow to young womanhood there. By the time they are ready to assume their complete responsibilities as wives, they are completely adjusted to the man and to their role in his life. I have heard these make the happiest wives. Perhaps, in a way, Della was like that. Before she could love as a wife, she had to love as a child. It's getting late, Alexis. Shall we prowl all night, or shall we stay here?"

"We shall stay here," he said. "We have come far enough today. Goodnight, Hellbent." And with that he settled himself in a corner and I, diagonally across the room from him, watched him glow in the dark.

CHAPTER 15

AT THE FIRST FLUSH OF DAWN, when the shadows deepened and the eastern side of Earthly objects glowed like burnished copper, Alexis arose and stretched.

"Did you rest well?" I asked.

"Peacefully," he answered, smiling down on me.

"Alexis," I said then, "you must be very, very old . . ."

"Old?" he said. And then he laughed. "Time is only an interval in the Scheme of Things, Hellbent. The winking of an eye, the snapping of the fingers. A little scoopful out of eternity. But, yes. In your limited way of measuring, I should be considered — " and he paused to chuckle again, "very old. I have no way of knowing how old because of course I have no way of measuring."

I paused, trying to grasp the magnitude of eternity, which could not be grasped at all. "You must have been sent on many missions," I said. "To many different lands . . ."

"Yes," he said, nodding.

"Can you tell me about any of them?"

"No, Hellbent. That I cannot do."

"Think of it," said I. "To be Timeless, to possess all that knowledge and understanding and experience . . . Why, you wouldn't even have a language barrier, would you?"

He turned another half smile on me. "No. Have you forgotten what happened on the day of Pentecost among your own kind? Besides, He *is* the Word."

He went from room to room in the empty house then and I got up and tagged along behind him, explaining as we went. "The kitchen, Della and Non Regenerate's room, my room. . . . My room was green and tan, as I recall. There were three large bookcases . . ."

"You enjoyed reading?"

"Not right at first, but later. At first I was like a young animal let out of a cage. I wanted only to run and leap with exultation."

"You left off attending the churches altogether?"

"Of course! We romped and played and joked. I finished high school, I took two years of journalism, I went to work on the newspaper . . ."

"And all that time you gave no serious thought to Him?"

"I gave no thought at all to Him. If He was the Governor of the first seventeen years of our lives, then not much could be said for His governing. And if, as you are about to point out to me, He was not permitted by my parents and their relatives to be the Real Governor because they did not adhere to His teaching and training, then I could only conclude that He must not be as Powerful as the Guide Book would lead one to imagine. And if the Guide Book was correct and He *was* Powerful, but only refrained from using His Power until such time as they should use their obedience, then I could not see Him as very Loving. For what of Della and me? And as Non Regenerate pointed out, there were gods and gods and gods. The Greeks had gods, the Indians had gods, and even the ancient Israelites, His own selected people, adopted gods from the heathen nations around them, and whatever came of them all?"

"Well, nothing," said Alexis, "except — "

"That's just it! *Nothing* came of them. And what, so far, had come from *Him*? Misery, neglect — "

"I see," said Alexis. "You chose to ignore Him."

"Well, He certainly seemed to have ignored Della and me. But, no, 'ignore' is not the right word at all. To 'ignore' a thing is to admit its existence and then refuse to take notice of it. I chose, rather, to deny His existence altogether."

Alexis stopped walking and looked out through a dingy window, his back toward me. "You became an atheist?" he asked.

"No. Not at that point. If I became anything at all, it must have been agnostic. I simply gave up on all sides and decided that nothing was, after all, really known or knowable."

"And Non Regenerate. Was he agnostic also?"

"No. More atheistic, I think. He dismissed supreme beings in general as being rather mythological — variable creatures born out of men's minds to defer facing the finality of death. If he leaned toward any explanation, it was scientific."

"Evolution, then?"

"More or less. Though he preferred just to leave the whole enigma to chance. 'Let us consider what we do know,' he used to say, 'and appreciate what is positive.' "

"And this meant, of course, that he was a happy, successful man, in love with his wife?"

"Yes."

"And what of fulfillment?"

"For him this was fulfillment."

"I see," he said. "The great mirage."

"The great mirage, Alexis?"

"We shall come to that later. Right now, how long did this season of atheism entertain your thinking and what, eventually, changed it?"

"Well, it's difficult to say exactly how long the general concept of atheism dwelt within the back of my mind for we never really know how deeply rooted a belief or 'sense' is. I should say that I began to change when I began to work among people and, for the purpose of writing about them for the newspaper, noticed that they behaved in certain set ways, or that they conducted themselves by certain set standards, regardless of race, color or creed. When I studied wars, for instance, I noticed that the majority of people felt that the one side was wrong and that the other side was right. And yet, who was to say that wrong was wrong or that right was right? Why could it not all be reversed?

"Though I was too young at that time to be personally involved in World War II, I found myself wondering why the Allies were right and Hitler was wrong. I wondered why *I* felt such a keen sense of right and wrong. It could only be explained in the fact that Hitler came upon the world with an ideology contrary to the innate sense of right and wrong which most other people possessed."

"I see," he said. "You stumbled upon the moral law."

"Yes. And once I had stumbled upon it, I could not keep from wondering where it came from. Each of us was *born* with a conviction that some behavior was good and some behavior was bad. Often the behavior itself was the *same*, but the motivation made it either good or bad. For instance, if I saw a dog bite a child and I kicked the dog, that was good. He had it coming. But if I saw the same dog sitting on the grass sunning himself minding his own business, and I walked over and kicked him, that was bad. The act was the same, but on the one hand it was a good act and on the other hand it was a bad act. So, if each one of us was born with this sense of right and wrong — or moral law, as we have called it before — then it had to come from someplace. It couldn't all be coincidence, not in all the creatures on Earth."

"And that was when you decided there had to be some outside force?"

"Yes, in a way. I decided, let us say, that there was a 'force.' I did not yet decide that it was an *outside* force. I think, rather, that I recognized the importance and pre-eminence of the mind."

"Idealism, then?"

"Only to a degree. And only for a while. However, by

that time I was working with people during the day and reading half the night. I dabbled with evolution. Sometimes Non Regenerate and I talked it over, though he clearly preferred to leave the whole mystery to itself, and I clearly could not make much logic out of it. The 'beginning,' according to any evolutionary theories I could find, was never reasonably explained at all. The 'fragment' which eventually became Earth had to come from someplace. If two minerals met in a mud puddle and, together, sparked Life — or whatever is loosely supposed to have happened — then the minerals and the mud puddle had to come from someplace. As to development into man, there had to be some kind of 'drive' — just as men are now driven to become better, to know more, to live longer. And if there was 'drive,' there had to be some kind of mind. If there was some kind of mind, which sought betterment, then that is supernatural and not mere material development at all. And if there was no mind, then how could matter have 'drive' and develop in the first place? No matter how I mulled it over, it came down to having to block one's mind at a particular point and not ask beyond. I could not accept that."

"I agree," said Alexis. "But if not evolution and not totally idealism, what then? Pantheism?"

"No, not pantheism, because pantheism did too good a job of controverting moral law, to my way of thinking. If all the universe were of itself a supreme being, composed of all existing laws and forces therein, then what becomes of the inborn sense of good and bad? Nothing would define good, and nothing would define bad. Both would simply exist and be included in the whole bundle. There would be no 'taking sides,' but simply the recognition that that type supreme being would embrace everything and you might conclude whatever you liked about good and bad, and the universe wouldn't much care because the whole bundle would still be the whole bundle, above and beyond small distinctions."

"You seem to have investigated and rejected beliefs at a rapid clip, Hellbent."

"No, it wasn't rapid at all, Alexis. It was several years. One thing led to another, one study to another."

"I see. But the studies always seem to end with the return to the moral law, is that right?"

"Yes. I suppose because the moral law was a thing inside myself, which existed and persisted."

"Did you decide it might have been controlled by two forces? A good and a bad?"

"Yes. But on the other hand, badness is only perverted goodness, isn't it? That is, everything is good until someone uses it in a bad way. Money is good, for instance, unless it is used to evil ends or unless the desire for it should drive one to commit evil deeds. Food is good unless, as we mentioned before, we over-indulge or else make ourselves nuisances over it. Clothing is good unless we permit our appearance to make us slaves of pride or debt. So, it would seem to me, that 'good,' as such, is really the origin and that 'bad,' as such, is the parasitic offspring. Which meant that I could only agree to *one* 'force,' and that a basically 'good' force."

"Deism, then?"

"No, because the sense of moral law was certainly not beyond the range of human experience. It was *within* human experience. And all the time, Alexis, I was reading history books, too. If it had not been for the history books, I could possibly have stopped at theism. But the history books gave names and places. And the names and places tied in with the Guide Book."

"You completed the cycle then: away from the Guide Book, down through the abyss of rejection, and up the ladder of logic to the Guide Book again. That was when you believed and accepted?"

"No, it was not all that simple. If I believed at all (and I know now that I did), I was far too rebellious to accept. Instead, I built walls against that side of my mind and said, as did Non Regenerate, 'Think no more. Dismiss it all. Live with and for Known Quantities.'"

85

"I see. And that got you into real trouble."

"Yes, Alexis. Real trouble."

"We shall take it up then, Hellbent. But let us do so in another place."

And with that we left the empty little house and proceeded down to the end of the sidewalk and out to the dirt road.

CHAPTER 16

THE SUN HAD CLOUDED OVER now and the sky was murky. Thunder rumbled in the distance, and the earth smelled damp and expectant. Alexis walked on down the country road paying the weather no heed, his hands clasped behind him in a strangely professorial posture. Presently the wind came up, turning the leaves perpendicular in its conical route. The grass, bright green in this dismal aura, dipped and swayed. Still Alexis trudged on, glancing now and then at a barn, a farm house, cattle hovering watchfully. I noticed that his raiment went unstirred save for little wisps of luminescence flickering off and disappearing.

Then the wind died down and the rain began. I felt the coolness of it but not the wetness, for it went right through me. I turned to Alexis to comment but saw that the raindrops as they came against his radiance turned to liquid pearls, rolling gently off him and, when they left the penumbra of his illumination, becoming again transparent and sinking softly into the ground.

"Alexis," I said with a surge of affection, "you are quite beautiful. I should like to see you as you really are."

He sent me a portion of a smile. "Perhaps I would frighten you," he said, "if I appeared as I really am."

"Which is intended to imply that I am not ready for that much reality?"

He looked amused. "Do you know where we are going, Hellbent?"

"Of course! I have driven down this road many times. Though not for many years, you understand. I was much younger then."

"But you were old enough to know better."

"Not necessarily, Alexis. A child may be told that stealing is wrong, but, when he grows up and sees adults getting away with it in all sorts of legal and political ways, he may come again to the end of believing that either he was wrongly instructed to begin with or else that the mode by which one accomplishes a feat determines whether or not the feat may be acceptably accomplished."

Alexis grunted. "That sounds rather as if you are using your parents' sins to justify your own."

"We've been all through that, Alexis. Why do you hark back to it at all? You know perfectly well neither Della nor I had any wish whatever to ape our parents' sins. I told you that the sin had to do, in a sense, with Him — though I would have denied it at the time."

"But you did substitute fornication for religion, Hellbent, just as your parents substituted adultery."

"Not for religion, Alexis. And not as my parents did. Possibly they made that kind of substitution, flinging the one out the door in favor of the other. However, my mistake had to do not with *culmination* but with *quest*. And not with religion, but with Him."

"I see. You had got beyond right and wrong, then, and were groping for answers at any cost."

"Something like that. I told you I had read of other cults and had, one by one, dispelled them. Starting from the Guide Book, when Non Regenerate took me in, I walked in the opposite direction until, like a man walking around the Earth, I saw outlined in the distance the point from which I had started. I couldn't stand what I saw because of all the obvious entailments. I seriously tried to listen to Non Regenerate, to 'forget it all,' to 'live for Known Quantities.' But what was right for him was not right for me. I still nurtured within myself the thing called moral law."

"In other words, he was married and you were not. Well? Could you not have gotten married? You were endowed with more than average attributes."

"I didn't want to get married! That was the last thing in the world I wanted! Hadn't I seen enough of that?"

"But Della — "

"Della was a female and, as you suggested, badly enough in need of paternal care to grow into all the rest of it. I was a male who reasoned and read too much and to whom the thought of chaining myself to one creature, exposing myself to continual debate, was suffocating. No, Alexis. Definitely not. The satisfaction was far outweighed and trampled into the dust by the impending dissatisfaction. Still — "

"Yes, Hellbent?"

"Still — that yearning was inside me for *something* — I didn't know what . . ."

"I suppose that with each new cult you hoped you would find completion and contentment?"

"Yes, but I never did. No intangible exploration or tangible acquisition gave peace to the longing. No sect, no sunset, no food, no drink, no accomplishment (for by that time I had begun to toy with writing fiction as well as fact) — *nothing* anesthetized, except momentarily, the bittersweet longing."

"But you would not permit yourself to believe that the longing was for Him?"

"Certainly not! After a while the longing had grappled with the moral law until, like a man possessed with demons — feverish and demented, I discarded the one on the basis that it had no logical origin and channeled the other in the wrong direction."

"You discarded moral law and channeled the longing into the oblivion of the great mirage: the obscene depiction that mortal lust consummates Holy Desire!"

"It does no good to scold, Alexis. What is done is done. Besides, if it meant the further exoneration of my guilt, I would not undo it. And never having been truly human, you can only look at these things objectively. Holy Desire, as you call it, easily loses its identity and permits itself to be interchanged with a multitude of other cravings. It remains Holy only by disproving and casting away, and in the end, all its stand-ins. In its maturity it becomes so acute, at times so agonizing, that it is more than 'nearly physical.' It *is* physical — almost shamefully so."

"Ah, ah!" warned Alexis. "Never say 'shamefully' of that particular Desire. Because you confuse it with what you know of longing in physical ways, it may *seem* to you to have some similarity. And perhaps it does in that He would whet your appetite for more and better things. However, it is not 'shameful.' Nor, for that matter, are any of your other longings, as you have pointed out yourself, as long as one keeps to the Guide Book. There are any number of things He has set before you for your happiness and satisfaction, such as you have listed: food, drink, beauty, love, success — to name a few. Now, none of these is intended to satisfy Holy Desire for Him, but only to give pleasure along the way. Furthermore, acute as you say Holy Desire has been, you have known only a smattering of what Divine Fulfilment can be. But then, we are talking as if you wished to spend eternity above, and you do not, so let us get back to here and now."

He went on, his face expressionless but, somehow, by that very quality, publishing self-satisfaction. I felt annoyance in place of my former affection.

"Do not set juvenile traps for me, Alexis," I muttered. "And it's all well and good for the rain to roll off you like so many lustrous gems, but what of me? I am cold and I shall catch — "

Alexis laughed aloud. "Your death? How can I consider you other than a child when, like all humans, you revert to acting like one? But do not be dismayed. It is as it was intended. Here, now. Is this where she lived?"

We stopped by the side of the road and looked toward a shingled farm house with a red brick porch. A German Shepherd spotted Alexis glistening in the gloom and protested loudly, but the woman inside the house drew back the curtain and, seeing nothing, told him to be quiet, he could not go out in the mud or he would track the place.

"Yes," I said. "She lived here. She was a pretty girl. Blonde, blue-eyed."

"Did you love her?"

I hesitated. And then said, "No. I think I was incapable of human love. Either incapable or unwilling to settle for it. I often thought Della was incapable, too, but she made the try — and pretended a little."

"The girl who lived here. Did she love you?"

"No. Not really. You will see."

"But if neither of you loved — "

"She was incurably romantic, Alexis. In love with love. In a way, she was like me. She hoped one thing and reaped another. I say 'incurably,' but perhaps, properly guided, she might have been aimed toward the road leading to Him. I was no proper guide and later, when I might have been, it was too late. We were by that time in the wilderness, as far as making another start."

"Another physical start, Hellbent. But what of spiritual?"

"She would not go back."

"She was a Believer, then?"

"In the beginning, she said she was not — possibly only to please and appease me. Later, when she found out about the child, she said she was. Later still, she again said she was not. I have always suspected that, deep inside, she was but she did not usually like the pattern He set before her so she parried."

Alexis nodded. "How old were you then, Hellbent?"

"Twenty-seven."

"And she?"

"Twenty-two."

"Had you known her long?"

"No. Her family had moved here quite recently." ·

"How did you meet?"

"It was on a day like this. Della had ordered a chicken for Non's birthday dinner, and I volunteered to drive out and get it for her when I came from work. The Transient family sat at the table having dinner. They were a large family — six boys and one girl. Folly was her name. They were all farmers and Folly was kept at home to help her mother. Like me, she lived in an untenanted sphere of searching. Though at first we knew only an immediate physical attraction. While the rest of them went on with their meal, Folly waited on me. She came out to the back porch to get the chicken and then, as she took the money and handed me the parcel, she said, 'We're new here. I don't know anyone. It gets lonely . . .'"

"I see. Her parents voiced no objection?"

"No. Though they hinted that they had little use for men who wore white collars and sat behind desks."

"Did you ever lead her to believe you would marry her?"

"Never. I made the opposite very plain."

"But she still wished to pursue the relationship?"

"She was more insistent than I. When several days passed without my seeing her, she would call Della. Della used to laugh, 'That little farmerette will have you at the altar yet . . .'"

"Did it occur to you that her generosity might have been a snare?"

"It did, but I told her repeatedly that marriage was out."

"And how long did the attachment last?"

"Less than six months. And the latter half of that I spent disentangling myself."

"It appears you were not at all happy in the role of a lover."

"Not at all. It was only a sham for a better thing."

"Then why did you continue even as long as you did?"

"Habit — and lack of the 'better thing.'"

But suddenly the sky flashed glaring white. There was a sharp crackle directly behind us followed by the groan of falling timber. I turned quickly, in time to see a gigantic oak come crashing down upon us. It passed completely through me, bouncing as it settled to the earth, and, to my utter amazement, splintered and fell apart as it hit Alexis so that he, in effect, drilled a hole clear through its bulky trunk!

"Alexis!" I cried. "Are you all right?"

But he stood there in the midst of the foliage with the bole surrounding him hip-high and said, as if I were a simpleton, "Of course. Perhaps now you will come to understand a bit of matter and substance."

"Shall I help you out?" I asked, fluttering about uselessly.

"You?" he asked. "Who have no resistance to a raindrop or a summer breeze? Do not be ridiculous." And the next thing I knew he was out of the tree, across the fence and halfway up the hill to the barn.

"Velocity of a hurricane, Hellbent! Do not stand there gaping! In no time the place will be swarming with humans and we shall not be able to hear ourselves think. Come along to the stable and let us continue there."

But before I did a thing about it, I was already at his side.

CHAPTER 17

WE SETTLED OURSELVES IN THE HAYLOFT and watched, for a while, the activity on the road below. The woman came from the house with the German Shepherd barking at her heels. A man ran out from the garage in back. A car approaching from the opposite direction skidded to a halt as it came to the huge obstacle, completely blocking the way. Two men and a woman got out and slogged through the mud to inspect the oak. The three men tried giving it a shove, but it would not budge.

"The strangest thing," we heard one of them say. "That hole right through the middle of the trunk . . ."

"Must be where the lightning hit," one woman volunteered logically. "Though it looks as if it had been done deliberately . . ."

"Make a nice yard ornament," the other woman suggested.

"*If* we ever get it out of the road!" a man added dourly.

Then one of them suggested telephoning for a highway crew, and they all plodded across the soggy lawn and up to the porch and disappeared inside.

"She will likely have some floors to scrub now," said Alexis, "and the poor dog will be the least of it."

I turned and looked at him, bright and cheerful with his legs crossed Indian-style. "How did you do it?" I asked.

94

"Bore right through the tree without so much as a scratch? And what did you mean of 'matter and substance'? Did you mean that you are of firmer stuff than the oak? But then how is it that you can walk through walls and doors without breaking them down?"

"Ah, Hellbent," he sighed. "Are we to have more of your pseudo-scientific interrogation?"

"Why is it pseudo-scientific?"

"Well, to you I suppose it is not. To you I suppose it is quite real. However, in the overall picture, known facts are few and theories are many. So many that the total aspect of what you call 'science' is to our species a snarl of presuppositions. It goes without saying that we are led to mild amusement when one of you makes some 'new' discovery that startles your planet."

"I see. We know very little, then?"

He shrugged. "You will discover what He allows, Hellbent. No more and no less. But from a celestial point of view the profusion of conjecture does give a pseudo-scientific cast, you must admit. Also no small irritation when the implication is made that He is behind the times!"

"Behind the times, Alexis? Do we imply that?"

"Absolutely! In your prayers you address Him as if you felt He could not possibly understand modern languages. In your ceremonies you employ archaic terminology. Your hymns cling to antiquated jargon. Your lessons are delivered to you sprinkled with borderline-obsolete expressions — "

"But, after all, Alexis," I interrupted, "all this stems from the Guide Book! Do not forget that the Guide Book is *old*, and that the lessons we are taught are concerned with happenings of long ago. If we somehow conclude that this dates Him, do not blame *us*. He 'always was' — "

"And *is now* and *ever shall be*," said Alexis. "Most of you seem prone to cling to His history but to disregard His *present* power and knowledge. You limit Him. But I rather suspect you like to think of Him as the Ruler of yesteryear and the

95

Ruler of tomorrow because you do not particularly care to have Him meddling in the today. To admit that the complexities which are one by one revealed to you in this age were but trivia designed by Him before the foundation of the Earth would, indeed, be frightening and perhaps even cause humans to take serious thought before launching into mischief."

I thought about it for a few minutes and felt a twinge of shame. "We are a rebellious, fidgeting lot, aren't we, Alexis."

He sighed, looking out at the rain. "Yes, Hellbent. Squirming, writhing, protesting. But then, what you are is not up to me except as I am so assigned. It does seem incredible that He should be so concerned over you, does it not?"

I drew a deep breath. "Yes, Alexis. It does. But — you never explained about the tree!"

"Oh, that," he said with a shrug. "You would not understand if I did. Let us just put it this way. I *wished* to go through the house, but I did *not* wish for the tree to fall on me."

"Do you mean it has, again, to do with 'free will'?"

"Something of that. Or you might say it was all an object lesson from above, designed to teach *you* His watchful care." And then he laughed so that I was not quite sure exactly what he meant. But since more teasing of the situation would have led only to more thought-twisting by him, I decided to leave it. In the end he would have directed my attention to the fact that all would be made perfectly clear when and if I acquiesced.

Recognizing his temporary victory, he fairly sparkled when he said, smiling, "Let us get back to Folly Transient. You have given me the impression that it was a rather one-sided relationship, with Folly making most of the overtures. Is that the idea you wished to convey?"

"Not necessarily, Alexis. I do not intend to shift the blame, nor even place it. She was a receptive girl certainly — and more so. However, if I had been a different sort, she might have been a different sort."

"But the whole affair, at best, was spasmodic and more one of retreat than pursuit on your part?"

"Well, probably because I realized sooner that this was not what I wanted."

"I see. But since her original quest was of a different nature, she was deluded longer."

"Yes. That is, she *thought* her quest was different — that she searched for the perfect, story-book kind of love — but I have come to wonder since then, Alexis, if all humans do not really seek a supernatural satisfaction. He made us that way — for Himself."

"Ah, for Himself, Hellbent, but still distinct individuals. His ultimate goal for you is union to Himself for *your* sake, so that He may overflow, spreading glory and happiness through you for eternity. But then, you do not want that. So get on with the consequences of your association with Folly. You finally broke the thing off completely?"

"Yes — and no. I finally stopped seeing her altogether, but then she came to Della with the news that she was expecting a child."

Alexis shook his head. "A logical outcome. How did Della react?"

"Badly, I'm afraid. You see, Folly was still there when I came from work. Della was crying. 'How could you, Willful?' she kept saying. 'After the way we were brought up, how could you?' Folly did not cry at all. She only smirked. 'You will have to marry me,' she said. 'Now you will have to marry me.' I could not see that making another mistake would in any way obliterate the first. The child would have suffered for our discontent. I refused. I agreed to assume all financial responsibility and, indeed, make a sizable settlement. She was nearly ready to accept that when Non Regenerate returned home. He was the one who upset the whole plan."

"How was that?"

"You will remember that I told you Della shrank from the involvement of motherhood. Non Regenerate, far from

97

forcing the issue, never even brought it up again. Nonetheless, it was obvious by the attention he paid other people's children that he privately hankered after a family of his own. He was thirty-six now and doubtless felt a sweep of desolation at the incompletion of this facet of his life. Folly's predicament seemed made-to-order. He immediately asked, 'What of the child? Are you all so concerned with personal encumbrance that you forget the plight of the child?' Della was dumbfounded. 'Surely,' she said, 'you cannot mean to infer that *we* — that *I* —' 'What else?' he asked. 'Do you think I could stand by and see this child given to strangers or put in an orphanage? Any more than I could have turned Willful out when he was alone and underage?' 'But,' said Della, 'that was *different*. Willful was older —' 'And needed me so much the less!' cried Non. 'There is no other way, Della dear. I could not sleep nights if we did not adopt this child. It's as if Providence sought to recompense. To overrule and override our pitiful human decisions . . . '"

"Mmm," said Alexis. "Strange talk from a man who professed to have no truck with Him."

"I thought so, too. But when I questioned him, he only said, 'Prescience is still science, Willful.' And he would not have his mind changed. It was the first time I ever saw him so unswerving."

"And Della? What of Della?"

I sighed. "Della wept and worried, died a thousand deaths and nearly wished the child dead as well rather than to face what she felt was the possible ruination of its life. Watching her suffer, I came close to agreeing to the marriage, but I knew with certainty that that would have destroyed the child. In the end, I sided with Non. 'You have been happily married for over ten years, Della,' I reasoned. 'I am sure that you and Non would make fine parents, since he wants this so much. Perhaps later you will even decide to have other children.' But she turned on me in a rage. 'You!' she screamed. 'After all our misery, all our clawing our way up from the pits of agony, you went out and did this heinous deed . . .' But she had grown from childhood to womanhood and she now understood a bit of the ingredients of love — consideration, self-sacrifice. In ten years, he had never asked her for anything."

"She did concede, then?"

"Yes. She went away for a few months and stayed in the locale of the home to which Folly went. When the child was born, Della and Non made all arrangements and brought it home. Folly and her family moved off to the next county."

"The child's name, I take it from your parents' relatives' conversation, is Vicie?"

"Yes. That is, her middle name is. The moment Non set eyes on her he said, 'We shall name her Bonny!' But Della, more fearsome, said, 'We shall call her Victim.' And then, her face crumpling, 'Poor Victim! Poor little Victim . . .' And she gathered the child up in her arms and rocked it to and fro, murmuring her love."

Alexis drew a deep breath. "She did succumb to the child, then?"

"Succumb?" I laughed aloud. "She adores Vicie! She fusses and coos and yearns over the child to this very day! She protects and defends and cherishes her. To harm the child is to tamper with a tigress!"

Alexis chuckled. "But they did name her Victim?"

"They named her both. Bonny Victim. But Della chose to call her Vicie and Non, enthralled by his sudden fatherhood, soon fell in with the nickname. Later, when Non and I both had an inkling that Della was seriously considering adding to the family, it became abruptly necessary for her to submit to surgery. Vicie then became more important than ever to them."

"And how did you feel toward her? Did you remain in the same house with them still?"

"I loved her, of course," I said quietly. "I felt sick over the gossip spread by my parents' relatives. But I could not wish to do any differently. Vicie's childhood was idyllic. And, yes, I moved into an apartment by myself. The relationship was too close. I sometimes found myself wanting to display parental affection. For Non's sake, I moved out. It was easier to remain objective as the 'visiting uncle.'"

"You went back to your books."

"Yes. Among other things. But look. They've cleared the tree away and the sun is coming out again . . ."

"All right," he said understandingly. "We will give it a rest." And then he added. "Loneliness is not an easy thing to discuss. . . ."

CHAPTER 18

THOUGH IT WOULD HAVE BEEN much simpler, to my way of thinking, to have employed his miraculous powers of extracting us from the hayloft, Alexis decided to go down the chute to the ground floor.

"You will break a leg," I warned.

But he laughed, "Don't be a fool, Hellbent. Come along!" And, like a silver streak, down he went. There was nothing to do but follow.

It proved a disappointment to us both. I had the sensation of no sensation at all, and Alexis shrugged, "What idiocy, after universal transposition."

I could not help smiling. "Do you never tire of being what you are, Alexis?" I asked.

"My, no!" said he. "I must confess to impatience that you humans do not always appreciate what you are, though. For the real joy of existence lies in discovering what He wants us to be and then in being that thing."

"Do you know what He wants me to be, Alexis?"

"Why, of course. And so do you."

We were by now out in the sunlight and Alexis made a game of jumping over the puddles, though I could not see why — for the mud never clung to his sandals or feet but splashed away, with opaque iridescence, and became, once more, mud.

"Being one of His children is not the lark you like to make out, Alexis, for it is necessarily a two-way proposition as I have shown you. To love Him is to obey Him, and to obey Him is to love fellow Believers."

"A bit more than that," said Alexis mildly, missing a puddle and sending a spray of jewel-like liquid behind him. "Change it to 'fellow beings.' That was the idea, you know. To love one's neighbor as one's self."

"Ah! But supposing I do not care much about myself? Which, actually, is the case. Then I do not have to care much about my neighbor, do I? If I dislike what I say and do, may I not also dislike what he says and does?"

"But of course! The rule says *love*, not *like*. You do not have to *like* him or palaver untruths if the man is evil. However, bear in mind that even while you were not particularly pleased with yourself, you did see to it that you ate regularly and that you were sheltered and protected. This is what the rule means — that you should feel and do the same for him, even if he is not particularly likable. That is what He does for you. After all, He is love."

"But He is also *truth*. When a whip needed to be cracked, He did not refrain from cracking it, I've noticed."

"But certainly, Hellbent! Do not confuse real love with superficial sentimentality. If He had been only sentimental, He could have waived men's sins, but because He truly *loved,* He died to bridge the gap between men and Himself. This was no wishy-washy action of a coward!"

"It *was* an action, then, His love, and not a feeling?"

"Absolutely! And in this He set the example for you, that you can only love truly when you are willing to put love into action. This does not mean that you should be deaf and blind to other beings, but simply that you must, in truth, be willing to deal with them as you would deal with yourself or have them deal with you."

"I see. And this, in turn, ties in with forgiveness? If we would expect Him to forgive us, we must forgive others. Likewise, we must forgive others as we would like them to forgive us. It all comes back to being triangular, the relationship between Him and us. He is to us as we must be to one another and, thereby, to Him."

"Yes. That is the general idea. And it should follow quite logically that since He became a Living Example of Love and Truth that opposition to these should be counted most serious."

"Sins of the spirit!" I said jubilantly. "But those are the sins, the hideous sins, which make His plan so unbearable! If only Believers — "

"Now, now," said Alexis. "He is also Righteousness *and* Hope. Which includes not only other types of opposition to Him, but also the way out."

"Nevertheless, Alexis," I argued, "according to His very words in the Guide Book, He did more denouncing of the self-righteous than condemnation of the physically sinful."

"I have never disputed that, Hellbent. But I get the feeling now that you should like to see your parents' relatives in hell and that you yourself should like to take a turn at living above, and *that* is really judging. Observing facts is one thing, but wishing — "

"Nonsense! I have no wish to change anything at all. Let them go above, and let me go below! You become more and more kittenish as we go along, Alexis. Try to remember that while I may be no fitting match for your maneuvering, I still have the wits of an adult human being and it will take more than a few debates to alter forty years of recognizing (and often bearing the brunt of) selfishness, deceit, hypocrisy, lying, cheating, misrepresenting, unreality — "

"Very well, very well! I can see you are becoming more and more edgy. Let us change the subject altogether. We are nearing town again. Was this not the street on which you rented an apartment? Or was it the one above?"

"You know perfectly well," I snapped, "it was two blocks up and a block and a half to the right."

"Oh," he said. "So it was." And then, with a twinkle in

my direction, he transplanted us to the doorway of the very building. "Up these stairs?" he asked innocently.

I could somehow not quell the forgiveness that flowed through me. "Alexis," I said sheepishly, "I am sorry. If only we could have met under different circumstances . . ."

"Ah, but then we would never have met at all, Hellbent. And, really, it is of no consequence. You cannot hurt me, you see. I am beyond all of that. But come. Let us go up."

We mounted the stairs to the second floor and walked to the end of the corridor. My apartment was on the left. A sign thumbtacked to the door read, "For Rent."

"It's locked," said Alexis, "but go on in." And, as before, we somehow continued walking and were through the wall and inside. Nothing had been changed. My clothes hung in the closet. My bookcases covered two walls.

"Poor Della," I whispered. "She will have to sort and dispose of all this! Somehow I never thought — Why, I should have done it myself before I — "

Alexis looked at me sympathetically. "That is the characteristic of sin, Hellbent. It never thinks of others. And the more centered upon consideration for one's self it is, the more pain and harm it brings to others. It occurs only because love of self prevails. That is why you have been told to love others as yourself. For if you truly did, sin could not occur."

I backed into the old rocker where I had spent what seemed endless hours pondering the condition of man and felt, for the first time, heavy. Alexis browsed about, reading book titles.

Finally he said, "Would you like to talk, Hellbent?"

"No," I said glumly. "I should like to leave this place."

"Leave this place? But you lived here for nearly twelve years! Why should you — "

"Because it reminds me — "

"Of what?"

"Of many things!"

"Then tell me about them."

104

"I don't want to!"

"All right, then. Just tell me the parts that do not seem unpleasant to you. Skip the rest, if you wish. Start at the beginning. You moved here while Vicie was still a baby, is that right? You were then twenty-eight. What did you do for the first couple of years?"

"You know what I did," I mumbled. "I read. I studied. I worked. I wrote a couple of books. Nothing eventful. It seemed more a period of – "

"Evasion?" he supplied quietly.

I jerked angrily. That is, my mind jerked angrily.

"If you want to call it evasion, call it evasion! It was just that the unrequited longing persisted and, search though I would – "

"Why do you wish to twist and contort, Hellbent? You found the answer, did you not? Right here in this room?" His voice was gentle, almost a whisper.

"No!" I croaked. "That is – *yes.* . . . That is, I found *an* answer, but not *the* answer . . ."

"How do you explain that?"

"Because the only logical answer was Him! I searched through billions of words written by hundreds of men covering thousands of years. I explored the deepest chambers of great minds and great souls, and the only feasible explanation to the existence of all things, the only possible hope of fulfilment lay in Christianity!"

"Well, then?"

"You seem to have missed the point of our entire sojourn, Alexis. Or else you do a fine job of pretending innocence! I set out to find beauty, and I found ugliness. I set out to find goodness and truth and mercy, and I found despicable behavior on all sides. I set out to find freedom, and I found chains. I wished with all my heart that I had not found any answer at all, for the longing itself was better than the false satisfaction!"

Alexis eyed me silently for a moment. "Not quite so," he

said then. "For you have seen that the longing itself leads to many iniquitous detours. As for the rest of it, surely you did not expect to have it all your way here on Earth, or there would be no point in going above, would there?"

"But it needn't be as far off from Him as it is, Alexis! I came to this inevitable conclusion that He was the Way, the Only Way, and I fell on my knees in this very room, before this very chair, and I cried, 'All right! I believe! I accept!' And then I went out into a world where the Glorious Creature to Whom I had just submitted my eternal being had become distorted and perverted until His Way no longer changed *lives* but simply *habits,* according to denomination and misinterpretation! Oh, I do not say that my interpretation is a mite better than another man's. I only say that changing an inflection here and there in the Guide Book to make convenient and self-acceptable what we already *are* is not the way at all! *His* Way involves radical change from the *inside out,* not merely social change totally external. You see, Alexis? You see why the next ten years were wrestling agony?"

"I see, Hellbent. And I agree there is a change in the quality of faith and, therefore, behavior. Nonetheless, you will remember that the Guide Book does say that your feet would be guided into the way of peace."

"And I suppose that's your way of saying that, if we aim in the right direction, our minds and hearts will become reconciled. Well, it didn't work! It just didn't work!" And then, when he only looked at me, "Alexis? Will I see them? Della and Vicie and Non?"

He smiled, but somehow it was more an expression of sadness than joy. "Yes, Hellbent. Tomorrow. But we still have a lot to accomplish today."

106

CHAPTER 19

WE AROSE THEN TO LEAVE the apartment.

"I suppose," I said coldly, "you are quite happy now that you have wrung from me the very thing I did not wish to discuss."

He sent me a glance saturated with surprise. "Why, I am always happy, Hellbent, and with a happiness that is not at all dependent upon yours — nor any other human's. You see, I am not on this side of the fence at all."

"I could go to hell and you wouldn't even care, Alexis?"

He elevated his tinsel brows. "I should do all that I could to prevent it, but your self-induced misery could in no way impair my utter joy."

"That doesn't even seem decent! That souls could be 'lost,' as the term goes, and that you could go on cavorting through eternity — "

"But, Hellbent! So may you!"

"That isn't the idea at all! The idea is that you seem to have no sorrow whatever — "

"But of course not! Why should I sorrow? Or why should any of you? You have been given a choice. However, if your choice were to lead you to hell, why should that hinder the happiness of the rest of us? Do you wish to control our bliss? Do you feel that the inhabitants of hell should have any sway up above? To feel that would be to feel that Lucifer should have got his own way and become the center of things! Surely you do not really want that."

"I don't know what I want. That is," I added quickly, "except peace. Which I am positive cannot be had among Believers."

"Well," he said, "we shall get to that. But for now, let us be off. Shall we jump out of the window?"

"Honestly, Alexis," I grunted, "must you ever be so playful? You know it will not be any more fun than the hay chute. Besides, you must have done it millions of times before. You don't have to impress me."

"Impress you?" he laughed. "If I really wanted to impress you, I would, with His permission, perform some major miracle and not toy with trifling frolic. Ah, no. You misunderstand altogether. I am filled with enormity of gladness and must express it. Come!"

And with that he ran to the window and gave a great leap. Out through the glass without disturbing so much as the dust on the sill and down to the ground with a feathery bound. Doggedly, I followed and felt nothing at all, except that where I had been *there* I was now *here*.

"With all that effervescence," I commented when we started down the street, "it's a good thing you do stay on the Right Side."

He chuckled, stepping over the cracks in the sidewalk again. "That is a certainty," he said. "For surely Lucifer, blast him, caused more evil than any *man* who has ever 'gone bad.' And surely man has caused more evil than any *animal* that has ever 'gone bad.' And so it goes. Our capacity for good also determines our capacity for bad. Not," he added with a glint of a grin in my general direction, "that you have failed to cause your share of sorrow and mischief."

I grunted aloud. "And that is why," I announced bitterly, "you are now about to take me on a round of the various churches I attended. To grub out my disputes and attempt

108

to change black into white by means of mystical magic and quicksilver controversy!"

"To the churches, yes," he said. "But not to alter any facts. You will see. Meantime, tell me what happened when you confessed to Della that you had become a Christian. I am presuming that you did tell her first of all?"

I sighed. "Yes, Alexis. I told her first of all. I went to their house on my afternoon off. (Truthfully, I stalled until then, experiencing such a commingling of confusion and embarrassment that I found it necessary to practice memorizing speeches!) When I got there, she was in the living room on the floor teaching Vicie to play with modeling clay. I sat down and we exchanged the usual amenities. Then suddenly she said, in her knowing way, 'You came to tell me something, Willful. You might as well come out from behind the bush and say it.' And I, turning red, I'm sure, forgot all the words I had memorized and simply blurted, 'Della, I have become a Christian.' I — I — "

"Yes, Hellbent? Yes — ?"

"I still scald with shame, Alexis, remembering the horror on her lovely face! She gasped. She turned white. Then she screamed and clapped her hands to Vicie's ears so that the child would not hear and begin to know. 'You will be with *them*, Willful!' she cried. And she started to weep loudly. 'You will be *one of them!*' I, too, realized the gravity of what I'd done. *I had separated our souls!* 'You can't, Willful!' she wept. 'You *can't!* You must somehow retract the belief — ' I remember how helplessly trapped I felt. 'Della,' I said, 'it's impossible. There was no alternative! It was the only logical solution — ' And then she screamed, '*Solution!* I should think it was the beginning of damnation to be condemned to the fangs and talons of our parents' relatives. I forgave you Vicie, but I cannot forgive you this! By this, you have placed an insurmountable wall between us forever!'

"I tried to explain to her that I would not join either of the churches of our relatives and that, if she liked, I would

109

not join any church at all. I tried to tell her that it was not a decision of feeling or emotion or foolish sentimentality but that it was one of cold, reasonable sense. I promised I would not come around preaching to Vicie or Non, and that I would in no way behave as our parents' relatives had, nor even mention my belief inside their house. But she only hissed, 'You will radiate with it! You will smell of it! They all do!' In the end, I left without her forgiveness."

Alexis shook his head. "Too bad," he said. "Too bad, Hellbent. What did you do then?"

"Well," I said, wresting my mind from Della's heartache, "my belief demanded that I set things right. I began with Folly Transient. I located her family after some searching and learned that she had married someone else."

"You actually intended to marry her at that late date?"

"Yes. I felt I should. I did not love her, but that was not really important — not as important as humans like to make out. For that kind of 'love' is, after all, an emotion which only triggers deeper, more important involvement. I felt that we could achieve contentment. Especially since I was willing to shoulder the blame and do the most part of the adjusting."

"I see. And did you talk to her at all?"

"Yes. Against her parents' wishes, I went to see her and to offer my apology — which was very little. Still, being the romantic she was, I thought it might make her at least fleetingly happy to know that I would have married her if it had been possible."

"How did she react to this?"

"Not well, Alexis. And she could not be blamed. It seems she had not told her husband of me or of the child. When she saw me, she cried, 'Get out! Before Dupe comes home!' There was nothing else to do but leave the past alone."

"Well, at least you tried. That is on the credit side. Not," he added, "that you want the credits. But, tell me, did Della remain aloof?"

"No. Non came home from work and they talked it over,

and he convinced her that I had always been a frustrated, hapless fellow and that it was not the human way to withhold forgiveness. She came to see me and said that under the circumstances I had outlined I might continue to visit them, but she also promised to do all in her power to dissuade me and to subvert what she called 'the Hostile Force.' But look, Alexis. We're by the school, and the children seem to be coming home to lunch . . ."

He shook his head. "No, Hellbent," he said quietly. "Do not get your hopes up. Vicie did not go to school today. Remember? You were just interred yesterday. That is, your corpse."

We went along silently then, while the children laughed and skipped about us. Presently Alexis said, "Let us go up this way, Hellbent." And we turned and went south.

CHAPTER 20

THE SIDEWALKS WERE DRYING NOW, and the air was hot and muggy. The children peeled off their light sweaters, and a man going down the street carried his suit coat over his arm and went about loosening his collar.

"It will rain again this afternoon," I said.

"Yes," Alexis nodded.

We came to a cement block building with a stucco front, and Alexis paused and admired it for a moment.

"I believe you attended this church for a while?"

"Off and on. That is, I always attended *some* church, but I didn't actually join any. First, because of the way we grew up. Secondly, because I had made the promise to Della. Thirdly, because of the inconsistencies between Believers' behavior and the Guide Book, as I have told you."

"I see. And yet you did not always live according to the Guide Book, Hellbent."

"No. But during these ten years of being a professed Believer, I certainly tried. Besides, Alexis, I have no grudge against a sincerely mistaken Believer. Nor against any Believer who honestly *seeks* to know His will and to *do* it. For instance, there was a Presence in the outer office of the High Registrar named Complete Trust. I could have lived compatibly and delightfully with his kind. And there were a few of them. But a very few in comparison to the ones bent on distorting

112

Him and the Guide Book to suit their own purposes and then insisting that their way is the right way and everyone else is in error."

"Of course, there is one thing you have not considered, Hellbent, and that is the immensity of the upper abode. Speaking in time-terms, it would be quite possible for you to exist for years without ever running across one with whom you had had a particularly chafing relationship. On the other hand, if you were waiting for someone in particular to arrive, you could seek him out without much ado."

"That may well be. However, you must agree that humans are, by and large, pretty much the same the world over. That is, they fall into categories of behavior. So, while I might not meet an individual I had actually known, I could still be exposed to his general *type* almost incessantly — which would be equally as bad as the individual."

Alexis shook his head and sighed. "You are stubbornly persistent in your conviction that there is no such thing as perfect happiness. Tell me this. How could perfect happiness *be* perfect happiness if we permitted unhappiness to exist therein?"

"That's just what I *have* been telling you!"

"Do you make Him out a liar, then?"

"I make Him out the opposite! Either He has given us free will or He has not. According to the Guide Book, He has. But if He revokes it when we discard our temporal husk and move above to dwell in His immediate presence, then it was not a gift at all but a loan. I cannot believe this could happen, for if He had wanted legions of robots, He could have created them. Instead, He created beings who could become His children — as you have said, Alexis, *by choice*. And if we have made the choices which place us in His immediate presence, why should He then remove the choice-mechanism and force us to become chattel? No, it cannot be that way.

"Since He abolished death, the upper abode must be an

113

extension and enlargement of a kind of life already established on Earth when we believe and accept Him. For, even as a human, I was in Him and He in me. This condition can only grow and wax greater and stronger when we go above. He will not make slaves of us."

"Very well," said Alexis. "Have it your way, and let us go on. Tell me how you came to attend this church."

As we walked slowly on down the street, I said, "In obedience to the Guide Book, I knew that I must attend and, since I vowed not to attend either of the churches of my parents' relatives, it was necessary to fellowship and worship elsewhere. This seemed like as good a beginning as any since they professed to live by His standards."

"And did they?"

If I had had a face, I would have grinned. "Yes and no," I said. "That is, they made a stab at it now and again, but perpetually recoiled with wailing and moaning. They were a niggardly bunch. I remember one man in particular — Even Swap was his name — who took one try at tithing. Oh, it was long before I started to attend their church, but to hear him tell it you would have thought it happened yesterday. It was, in fact, his favorite dirge. 'I tithed for six months,' he used to mourn. 'I was never rewarded. On the contrary, my wife got sick, my car broke down, the creek went dry, my horse died, the barn caught fire . . .'"

Alexis snickered. "I suppose you handed him a handkerchief?"

"Well, no, as a matter of fact. At first, armed with brotherly love, I tried to be patient and understanding and sympathetic. But after I had heard the lament six or eight times, I attempted to offer the explanation that we were not to expect monetary rewards necessarily and that if it were not for Him, there would be no wife or car or creek or horse or barn to begin with. But he was not the only one, Alexis. That church was full of them. There was Mrs. Parsimonious, for instance. Her main grievance was the way the Shepherd lived. '*He* drives a better car than *we* do,' she would say resentfully. '*His* house has been redecorated more recently than *ours* . . .' "

"But did they not provide the Shepherd with his house?"

"Of course. The parsonage was 'church property,' so to speak."

"And did they not recognize that he might have had a better-working budget?"

"My, no! Mrs. Parsimonius and her elite little group always concluded that the Shepherd was drawing too large a salary and that tithing was 'strictly Old Testament.' "

"What did you think about it yourself, Hellbent?"

"I thought, mainly, that all we have and all we are belongs to Him anyway, so there was not much point in setting up a fence at ten per cent. His selected people were told not to murder, for example, but He said Himself that we were not even to anger. Likewise, His selected people were told not to commit adultery, but He said in person that to look upon a woman lustfully was wrong. Applying the same ratio of comparison to the 'strictly Old Testament' instruction to tithe, it's easy to see the Guide Book was not carrying much authority. It is also easy to see that I was not looked upon favorably for my interpretation."

"Dear, dear. But surely *some* of the members did not begrudge Him?"

"Very few, Alexis. Oh, there were some who *tithed* — to the very fraction of a cent, as a matter of fact. And then they promptly made the fact known and attempted to set the pace for everyone else. One such example-setter was named Lime Light. 'Perfection,' he would declare, 'is best encouraged by performance. If we can see in others what we ourselves ought to be, we can make the change more readily. Now, I believe in obedience to the very letter and this is the way *I* figure *my* family's finances . . .' "

"Path of a cyclone," murmured Alexis. "Did he fail to realize that *his* idea of 'perfection' might not be true perfection at all? Or that where he stressed 'obedience to the letter' in one area, he might fall far short in another?"

"Humans never see themselves as others see them, Alexis. You know that. Besides, he was not really concerned with perfection. Only with putting on a show and using Him as the playwright."

"I see. You eventually drifted away then and began attending somewhere else?"

"Yes. Though I came back to this church now and again for as long as I remained on Earth."

We turned right at the next corner and proceeded west. The sun darted in and out between clouds as if trying to make up its mind whether or not to give in to the rain, one moment glistering and the next obscure. Looking down at the sidewalk to watch Alexis' intricacy in avoiding the seams, I noticed with some surprise that he cast no shadow. . . .

CHAPTER 21

AT LENGTH, THE SUN GAVE IN and so did Alexis, for we came to the end of the sidewalk and out onto a dirt path leading to the second church. This structure was severely plain and simply painted white.

"It would appear," said Alexis, "that these members gathered together to tend to business."

"Quite right," I said. "Their own and everyone else's."

He turned a pair of very round eyes upon me. "That was not nice, Hellbent. Taking Him seriously is no offense, you know."

"Of course not. But what they took seriously was *their idea* of Him. They were one great little group of correctors. Why, I had attended the church only once when Flinty Outlook cornered me in the vestibule and said, 'I am a fourth cousin to Folly Transient on my mother's side. Let me assure you, Hellbent, that the inner conflicts of such a way of life are not worth the stolen moments. There is only one way to peace with Him and that is by restriction. We were not meant to taste forbidden fruits or pirouette through life enjoying beauty or freedom. You will find that He is very jealous. Nothing must come before Him. The very *thought* of foolishness is sin. There is calm within only when we walk in sobriety . . .'"

"Howling winds!" said Alexis. "Did you never interrupt the man long enough to tell him you realized your mistake and had tried to rectify it physically and had confessed it spiritually? Besides, had he not read that a merry heart does the good of a medicine and a broken spirit dries the bones? After all, if he chose to quote — "

"I tried, Alexis, but he never heard me. 'Cutting all pleasures from life,' he went on, 'there is the real joy. Confining ourselves to everything we dislike, there is true compensation. That's the way He wants us to be — His Very Own . . .' "

"How did you extract yourself?"

"Well, actually I never did — until now. Each time we met it was the same. I finally stood there staring, and he usually ended with, 'I see you're getting the idea, Hellbent. Why don't you come to our home for dinner some Sunday?' "

"And did you?"

"Yes. Partly out of curiosity, I'm afraid, but mostly because I wanted to give myself every opportunity to come to love the man."

"He was married?"

"Oh, yes. He had twelve children."

"*Twelve?* But I thought — "

"Oh, he explained that to me, Alexis. He got me to one side and whispered, 'Foul business, parenthood. It's the one process I think He could have given a bit more thought to. But then, He did tell us to multiply . . .' "

"Well!" said Alexis. "Did he think *he* could have improved the plan?"

"Apparently," I said. "Though I never ventured to ask how. Would you like to go inside?"

"I am not sure that I would like to," he said, scintillating, "but since we are here . . ."

The floors were of tile, and the walls were painted gray. The pews were light oak, varnished to a sheen and with straight backs. Alexis sat in one of them and squirmed.

"Go on," he said. "Tell me of some of the others you met here."

I settled beside him and said, "Well, there was Mrs. Quite Unique. She had about the same views as Flinty Outlook, except that she didn't know about Folly. She started in on me about the books I wrote. 'We are to give all our best to the Master,' she said. 'We are to praise and glorify His name. We are to be separate. We are to have no association with the worldly. We are His chosen ones and we must keep to the rule of being exclusive. We must sever all outside contact. We must rend ourselves from temptation. Now, *I* have never been tempted to write. However, realizing that belonging to Him makes me special . . .'"

"Glazing sleet!" said Alexis. "According to the data furnished by the office of the High Registrar, there was nothing so shocking — "

"That's what I thought, too, Alexis — that I hadn't done anything wrong. Of course, she had never read anything I had written — nor troubled to ask my motives. She simply assumed that if money and reputation went with it, it had to be bad. And it was no use trying to explain to her that He came into the *world* to save *sinners*. She was even a trifle suspicious of the missionaries' occupations!"

"Let us be out of this place," said Alexis, shaking his head and showering sparks. "We can talk on the way."

It was drizzling when we started east again. Alexis immediately began to culture and repel seed-pearls of moisture. For several seconds we walked in silence and then I offered, "You might like to hear about Sharp Distinction. You remember I told you Mrs. Parsimonious of the other church was quite set against being governed by the Old Testament? Well, Sharp Distinction was quite set in the opposite direction. He felt that the only right way was circumscribed by unbreakable laws."

"The Ten Commandments, I trust?"

"Oh, no. Though he somehow derived that all of his own

laws were taken from those, I'm sure. And he was convinced that victory could come only when the entire world lived as he lived."

"Victory? What kind of victory?"

"I'm sure I don't know, Alexis."

"But what were the rules?"

"Mostly total abstinence from anything decorative, consumable or pleasureable. He was a highly accelerated projection of Flinty Outlook."

"Sounds formidable."

"He was. The criterion of his belief was to force his views on all the world, whether Believers or not. He was known to have assailed strangers on the street and snatched tobacco from their person. On one occasion he was said to have accosted a man coming out of a tavern and to have discoursed lengthily his version of temperance (which was complete restraint). I overheard him reprimanding a woman for her jewelry. And once he sent another weeping to the Shepherd's study because she 'painted her face' like Jezebel. He denounced all television, insisted that Christmas was a time of 'chastening the flesh,' and demanded psittacosic response from all members of his immediate family."

"Dear, dear," said Alexis. "What must the unbelievers have thought?"

"Probably," I laughed, "that the beginning of church knowledge was the fear of the brethren! For myself, I often wished I could have talked to Rahab. What an adjustment she must have had when she left Jericho and eventually married an Israelite. I wished she could have sat down with me and said, 'Hellbent, this is the way to get along with determined, blind pride . . .'"

"Yes," he said. "For all her being a harlot, her position in His presence is not one I would exchange for Sharp Distinction's — unless he mends his ways. As we have agreed before, the physical sins are bad but they arise from the human's fleshly nature. The sins of the spirit, however, come about by hellish means. Satan, may he writhe in chains of darkness, delights to inject into others the sin of his own downfall, and his methods are most insidious. For the moment any Believer feels, for any reason, he is closer to Him, more pleasing to Him, than others, he is immediately guilty of the cardinal transgression: pride. It may come about through attempted plainness, piety, self-denial, ignorance, incompetence — any one of dozens of ways of rejecting and disclaiming one's beauty, intelligence or talent — in favor of pretending humility."

"Really, then, that is one of Lucifer's cleverest tricks, isn't it? Confusing us on the issue of humility? By rights, we should take pleasure in whatever good things He gave us, but also be capable of taking equal pleasure in what He gave others. Instead, we cringe and cower and claim ugliness and uselessness, which really discredits Him."

"Exactly. And I have noticed that the same artificial values which caused men to feel 'correct before Him' thousands of years ago still persist today."

"Precisely what I have felt all along, Alexis, except that today we have drawn farther out of sight of Him and more set than ever on turning a deaf ear. The remedy does not seem to me to lie in inflicting unfounded rules and regulations upon each other but, rather, in aspiring to become the kind of being who will automatically live His laws without even being aware of them."

Alexis turned and looked at me. It was getting foggy and he appeared more radiant than ever cast against a background vapor.

"Too bad," he said, "that you have learned these many things and have no wish to become the beneficiary . . ."

But I turned away from him and answered coldly, "Don't get tricky with me again, Alexis. I am only playing politics — going along with you until such time as you shall agree to my release. Besides, can you be so imperceptive as to miss the whole point of everything I say? I am arguing *against them.* If that necessarily involves arguing *for Him* — well . . ."

"Of course," he said cheerfully. "Of course, Hellbent."

But it did seem to me he sparkled, and even emitted some kind of celestial music that was nearly tangible — like the far-off chorus of a thousand sopranos, tingling and reverberating until I was not sure I had heard them or *felt* them . . . Though I vowed the minute the sensation was past that I would certainly not ask! And he, bland and indifferent, walked on in that pedagogic pace.

CHAPTER 22

It was dusk when we came to the third building, which was no church at all, but the town hall. A rectangular frame construction sagging with age and thirsty for a coat of paint.

Inside, the lights were bright and a small orchestra, whose fiddler seemed to be the predominant personality, squawked out the beginning strains of a lively tune. The caller began his chant and multicolored cotton skirts swished past the windows as their partners whirled the ladies in a floor-pounding square dance.

Alexis and I stood outside in the evening mist and watched the action. "These are a gay bunch," he said. "Do you mean to tell me you had trouble with these?"

I laughed. "Of course not! These are not church members, and you know it. The church members only rent the place on Wednesdays and Sundays. The rest of the week it is let out to other groups."

"Oh? The church members plan to build their own edifice?"

"Yes. They've been planning to for twenty years."

"Twenty years, Hellbent?"

"Twenty years, Alexis."

"But I should think — in all that time — "

"Their membership is small. I doubt that they will ever have the money to build."

123

"Do they take in no proselytes?"

"Oh, yes. Now and again. But they generally drive them out."

"Drive them out! Hellbent, you had better clarify."

"Well, you see, Alexis, they are a quarrelsome bunch. Where the last church we visited wanted to conform outsiders as well as insiders (just in case the outsiders became insiders and, really, in the hope that their cruelty would somehow be interpreted as brotherly love and encourage this), this church left outsiders with a pleasantly sociable taste in their mouths until they became insiders. *Then* they released their venom."

"Do you mean they did not treat each other kindly?"

"Kindly!" I snorted. "Alexis, this is the one church in which I came to realize that I was not alone in my disillusionment. I would need all of both of our fingers and toes (providing I still had ten of each) to count the number of people who were hurt and who turned away, often with tears and sometimes with the resolution never to enter another such organization, regardless of Him."

"But what did they *do?*"

"Well, perhaps if I tell you about some of the members, you will understand. First of all, there was Bully Rude. He was a sizable man with a large family, and all of them acted the same. I have tried to work on committees with him. I recall one Christmas season in particular when several groups had arranged to use the hall on various days and each group, bit by bit, brought in its own needed equipment and set the paraphernalia around in different corners of the building . . ."

"You mean different *outside* groups?"

"Well, a few of those, too, but mostly inside groups. There were the various young people's parties to be held here, a get-together for the older folks, the pageant, and so on. As it happened, Bully was in charge of an adult dinner. 'Hellbent,' he said, 'I want the entire building gutted.' I looked around at the various preparations made by the other groups, some of them even covered over by blankets and drapes so as not to be conspicuous. I thought of the work the tykes had put into dressing the doll that was to be the Baby Jesus, making collars for the little chorus, robes for the little kings. Then there were the posters with excerpts from the Guide Book to be used by the older children, centerpieces for the tables of the older folks, cartons of hard candy to be given as prizes for the games for the young people. . . . I finally said, 'But where should I go with them, Bully?' 'Throw them out in the snow!' he said. 'Our group comes first!' It seemed strange to me that the *outside* groups managed without any of the church-member litter bothering them, so I could not see why he, being a member, should be so troubled by his own. When I mentioned this, he roared, 'I don't take any guff, Hellbent! From you or anybody else, see? What I say goes! I won't stand still and be bossed around! They had no business making plans so far in advance! Nobody shoves *me* to the center of the floor! I want the whole building, and if I want something, I take it! If they don't like it, *I'll* tell them off!' And he promptly opened wide the front doors and began tossing things out in the snow, mumbling all the while about 'wading in and showing them who is boss.'"

"Blazing meteorite!" gasped Alexis. "What came of it?"

"Well, amid his ranting, I salvaged what I could and stored it in my apartment, but some of the things — such as centerpieces — were beyond repair. In the end, about fifteen of the more sensitive souls left the church for good. Bully chuckled that 'he guessed he had shown them.'"

"But had he not read in the Last Judgment that his behavior toward fellow beings was the very same as his behavior toward Him?"

"Oh, he had read it, Alexis. He counted himself one of the scholars of the church and flaunted his Interpreted Guide Book. But, you see, the interpreter of his Guide Book clearly indicated that that passage did not apply to Believers."

"No!" said Alexis. "How can it be? If he were such a 'scholar,' why should he have need of an interpreter? And

125

by what right do men sift and categorize His Word? I will tell you, Hellbent, in all my eons of watching, and many times visiting, this planet, it has struck me sharply that humans prefer to 'cross reference' *around* Him, rather than to read and absorb directly what He has to say. Consider for a moment just *Who* He *is!* Why He ever selected to pay a call upon this muddy sphere at all is a mystery to me. But why humans insist upon tendentious elucidations is no mystery at all.

"They claim 'not to understand without help.' However, I have noticed they lean toward purchasing that Guide Book so foot-noted as to suit their own plan of salvation! Why do they not take Him at His Word? Any translation of His Word, but *His Word?* I think many of you would be shocked and surprised, and some of you, like Bully Rude, might grasp again that function of exercising faith, hope, love, peace. . . . For surely these should spring up inside you like new grass on an April morn. And without these, you know, He is quite handicapped when it comes to helping you. You must reciprocate in order for Him to give you all He has to give. And in order to reciprocate, you must know what His Instructions are. What they *really* are — as He plainly speaks them."

"I know, Alexis, I know. John put it very aptly. 'Love is of Him and everyone who loves is born of Him and knows Him. If, on the other hand, we say we love Him but hate our brother, we are liars. For if we can't love our brother, whom we see, how can we love Him Whom we have not seen'?"

"Of course, Hellbent, I could turn this application directly to you."

"Except, Alexis, that you have never heard me profess love, have you? I have only told you I believed because it was reasonable and logical and sensible. And if you want to go back to the reference that what we do to others is what we do to Him, then I should have to concede that since I do not wish to dwell eternally with Believers, I must likewise forfeit dwelling in His Presence. Have I ever denied it? But on the credit side, and just for the sake of argument, mind you, I believe you will find in my record that I tried to follow the Guide Book even to the extent of praying for those who despitefully used me and, in their way, persecuted me. I counted them my enemies and I tried to love them. It just didn't work."

"Perhaps you did not really trust Him to bestow the ability to genuinely love upon you."

"Oh, I trusted Him, Alexis. And I even forgave *them,* as I have told you. But each time I came near to loving them and could dismiss whatever it was they had done to me, they suddenly did some dastardly deed to someone more vulnerable than I and the whole cycle began again. Instead of trying to love people *into* their fellowship, the members of this church hated them *out!* Take Mrs. Savage, for instance. She was a do-it-yourselfer — forever snatching things out of other people's hands and appointing herself chairman. 'Nobody around here knows how to do anything right!' she has said to helpful newcomers. 'I have to do everything myself! Select the music, call and remind everyone of prayer meetings, staff meetings, board meetings . . .' In fact, she reminded me greatly of Aunt Priggish."

"I see," he said. "Religiously efficient but without love."

"Exactly. I remember one young woman who gently suggested to Mrs. Savage that it was more in keeping with His teachings to be patient and longsuffering and that she especially needed such consideration since she was, as she put it, a blunderbuss. Mrs. Savage turned on her and snarled, 'Don't you preach spirituality to me, you young snippet! I not only *keep* all the rules, *I made them!* '"

"Dear, dear," said Alexis. "What did the young thing do?"

"Took her membership card and went elsewhere. The last I knew she was still migrating from church to church. I met her on the street one day and she said, 'I do not seem to belong anywhere, Hellbent. I do not dress well enough for the one church. I have too great a sense of humor (even I, who seldom smile) for the other. I do not seem to belong . . .' "

"What did you say to her, Hellbent?"

Sheepishly I admitted, "I said, 'You belong to Him. *He* knows . . .'"

"Hmmph!" said Alexis. "You preach considerably better than you practice! But let us walk on and, tell me, were there still others?"

"Oh, yes. There was Mrs. Vicious. She could never forget what people had been, were now and, to her way of thinking, ever would be. If she heard of someone stepping outside the lines she drew, she went to their home and attempted to purge it. At meetings, she dropped little remarks about 'some people's pasts,' and the fact that anyone associating with 'such characters' would be indelibly marked for life. If you so much as had a fifth cousin who had once got a parking ticket, you were ostracized. In some cases, she even asked people to leave the church."

"Gusty gales!" Alexis breathed. "Was she so free from sin as to cast stones?"

I laughed. "I do not even have to answer that. You know. One of His basic teachings was that outward appearances counted for nothing. What went on in the heart was what interested Him."

"Yes," said Alexis. "The realism of spirituality, as you now know, is more important than the substance of things. This should be the human's natural mode of life. For then, you see, you would not class 'hope' as mere wishing but as lively expectation without all the self-justification which these people you have told me about seem to display. This life is, I admit, only a preview, and repentance should bring about a total change of prospect, as well as behavior. The trick, Hellbent, is for humans not to hammer away at Him in prayer to change everybody else, to change circumstances, to persuade Him against His will, but, rather, to submit to being changed yourselves so that you can safely receive power. I have seen this happen many times and there has been rejoicing among my own kind. *He* has not changed . . . But then,

I seem to be doing an undue amount of preaching myself. Let us get back to the process at hand. Are there other churches you feel we should visit?"

"*I* feel we should visit! Alexis, you know perfectly well that none of this was my idea. *I* had enough of these places when I was yet on Earth — which is why I am in this state now! The real question is, are *you* satisfied that none of this recounting-the-past therapy is going to alter my plea one iota?"

He drew a deep breath and looked down at his feet, stirring the fog as we went along.

"Patience, Hellbent," he said. "You shall see them to-morrow, as I promised. Though we have a few things to clear up first. But look! Is that a child's tree-house?"

I strained to see and said, "Yes, I think —" And then, "Alexis! Surely you don't intend —"

But even as I looked at him he soared upward like a shining beacon, making a path through the density and disappeared inside. An instant later his bright face beamed down upon me from a small, square window.

"Hurry along, Hellbent. We have a big day coming up."

There seemed no alternative but to follow in his flickering ray and join him.

"It is nice," he chaffed, "that you have no body that takes up Earth-space, for then we should have to decide which of us would sit upon the limb and which would occupy the nest."

"Humans," I grunted without amusement, "should change that expression 'I would not be caught dead' — in such-and-such a place. They might, *in fact*, be 'caught dead' in nearly any place. That is, if they are assigned to a Counselor like —" But then I stopped short and wanted to sit up very straight. "*Alexis!*" I gasped, peering at him. "That's *it! The others are counseled, too!* Aren't they? *Aren't* they —? Alexis? Alexis! Will you stop that silly grinning and twitching your nose? I know perfectly well you are not asleep! Why don't you answer me? Why *won't* you answer me?"

But he sat there like a huge, glittering jinni and said nothing.

When finally I settled down, he offered, "What difference would it make? If counseling is not helping you, why should it help them? Good night, Hellbent."

CHAPTER 23

THE SUN ROSE BRIGHT AND WARM, cutting through the mist and evaporating it. Shafts of light streamed in through the crude little open windows of the tree-house and fell upon a strange scene. Alexis, sitting cross-legged and occupying nearly the whole of the flimsy enclosure, was smiling gently down upon his own countenance. For there in his lap lay two stray cats, curled into furry balls and sleeping peacefully, and all about them, up and down his arms, thighs and shoulders, were perched birds of half a dozen different types and colors. Indeed, one very fiery cardinal sat peacefully atop Alexis' glimmering head! And all of them, whether sparrow, bluejay, starling, robin, wild canary or cardinal — including the yellow tiger cat and the gray angora — seemed to have absorbed his radiance until they fairly glowed. The yellow tiger cat stretched out its paw across the gray angora's neck and a bluejay resting on Alexis' knee reached down and rubbed his beak from side to side against the luminous outstretched paw.

"Alexis!" I whispered.

And at once they began stirring and chattering with uneasiness, very softly but aware there was an unseen presence. The gray angora opened its eyes and looked drowsily about. Alexis nodded slowly and tenderly stroked the battle-scarred ears.

"Why do they glow so?" I asked, still whispering.

He smiled. "Because they are close to Him — through me."

"You mean — that's His glory?"

"If you like. Or His love."

"They go against their own nature?"

"Of course! That is the whole idea!"

I sat staring at them, and a wild canary spread out its wings, ruffled its feathers and then hopped down from Alexis' wrist to the angora's upturned side and settled itself! The cat eyed it disinterestedly and turned away. The tiger, on the other hand, gave it a loving swipe with its tongue and then resumed dozing!

"Alexis," I whispered again, "does it happen like this with people? Up there?"

"People are more difficult," he said. "More determined to resist and cling to their own sinful way. Besides, I am not allowed to paint you any rosy word-pictures, Hellbent. You have to accept what you have read in the Guide Book and love Him enough to trust Him for the rest. You see, *you* are entitled to, and must, make the decision to trust. I have told you this before."

"But if He never revokes free will . . ."

"He has not revoked the free will of these birds and animals, Hellbent. The tiger may reach out and devour the canary. The angora may, with one cuff, fell the bluejay."

"But — they don't *want* to. Is that what you are telling me?"

"I am telling you nothing, Hellbent. Nothing of what happens when you pass beyond the office of the High Registrar. I am not permitted to. You have been given equal guarantees with all other humans, and you must trust or reject, according to your own will. I am at liberty only to help you on this side of His office. To clarify, explain, urge and assist."

"Well," I admitted, "you are very lovable, Alexis. If all the creatures up there were like you . . ."

"But we have mentioned before that your kind shall judge my kind."

"That doesn't mean they'll be any more lovable! Just that they'll have more practice by the time they get there!"

Alexis grinned and shook his head, causing the cardinal to flutter its wings. "Tell me, Hellbent. What of Della during your years of attending the various churches? Did she keep her promise to dissuade you?"

"Yes, Alexis. And I broke mine, I'm afraid. I did preach to her. At least — when she tried to subvert the 'Hostile Force.' "

"What methods did she use?"

"Arguments mostly. Non Regenerate would not stand silent for any other means."

"What kind of arguments?"

"Every kind. Sometimes she tried to appeal to my common sense, for instance. She would say things like, 'Honestly, Willful, with your level head, how can you fall for such nonsense? Assurance of salvation, indeed! Spiritual experience, my foot! Next you'll be seeing lights and hearing bells! Where *is* your head?' And another time she would say, 'All right, if you must believe something, then believe He was a great moralist. All right, so He really lived. Does that mean you have to go overboard? Do you have to become positively orgiastic about it? Believe what you want to, but stop demonstrating. Stop attending those miserable churches, and stop milling about with those schizophrenes!' "

"Moral teacher!" interrupted Alexis. "Did she not realize that anyone claiming to be what He claimed to be would be the very *opposite* of moral if the claim were untrue? Of all rationalization this concept of Him is by far the most *ir*rational! But then, I did not mean to break in. Please go on."

"Well, sometimes she got off in the direction of 'doing good' and of 'occupying excess energy in constructive ways.' She would say, 'Join some boys' club, Willful. Do your bit for humanity in that way. Become a leader for some underprivileged group. This will be more helpful to you than silly emotion and to the boys, too.' And on occasion she would be quite upset about it (especially if someone like Mrs. Savage took upon herself to call and 'set Della right'). She would say, 'This is nothing more than borderline insanity! Religious fairy tales! The bad are punished and the good are rewarded, but somehow it happens in quite the opposite way! Much more of this paradoxical idiocy and you will go quite mad and drive all the rest of us along with you!'

"Another time she would say, 'For goodness sake, Willful, get up on your hind legs and act like a male human being, will you? Look at the time you waste with those creatures. The world is passing by and all you are doing is indulging in juvenile fantasy while you sup with babes on milk toast!' Then again, she would take the opposite point of view and say slyly, 'Who do you think you're fooling? Do you suppose I, the legal mother of your illegitimate child, can be bluffed into thinking you have shut off all the valves of your manhood? One of these days another Folly Transient will come along and you will revert to being human again. Why try to pretend in the meantime that you are different? Why not admit what you are and live with it?' "

"Dear, dear," said Alexis. "She seems to have thought of everything . . ."

"Oh, she's a clever girl, all right. She still had a few others up her sleeve. One of the others was, 'After all, Willful, what has this really got to do with what you set out to find? You know perfectly well you are surrounded by hateful, hypocritical creatures so why pretend that the few who are decent sufficiently dilute the others? You know you are miserable. What has all this business of artificial rules and chains and spite to do with what you thought He was? Admit that you made a mistake and let's be done with it!' That argument came the closest to any of dissuading me, except for one other. Because, you see, it *wasn't* all I had hoped and I was only trying to be obedient as best I knew how, hoping inside

134

that it would get better — that I would progress as a Christian to that point of — well, actually, to that point of *becoming blind!* That's what it would have taken! If I had been blind and senseless and numb, if I had become tough-shelled enough to overlook cruelty and stubborn ignorance — well, in other words, if I were dead!"

"But you said this came the closest, except for one other. I should like to hear the other, but first I should like you to answer, quite honestly now, whether you do not *really* feel that, if you had *joined* some church, you would have given coexistence a more thorough try? Honestly now, Hellbent."

"Alexis," I said sincerely, "despite my promise to Della, I would have joined any one of these churches if just once I had ever felt really welcome or really closer to Him through their fellowship. Truthfully, after a session with someone like Bully Rude, I came away feeling like a demon! I did attempt to be 'active' in the churches I attended, and discovered I was not sturdy enough to withstand the tactics. On one occasion I was months doctoring an ulcer! And if you are about to point out that I never learned to lean on Him, then I will have to counter with the fact that the schools I attended taught me little more than self-preservation and, in the end, even that proved meaningless.

"I have been totally disillusioned, Alexis. Besides, I do not really believe the individual Believer is the solution to the present coldness and distance from His teachings. What is needed, more than individuals straggling in together, is a totally cleansed and rejuvenated comradeship, witnessing *lovingly* to each other and the whole Earth. This, as far as I can see, can only come about when Believers see Him as He really is and not as they like to think He is or as they have been erroneously trained to think He is. They can receive this sight only from Him and only by permitting Him to give it to them. They will know when they have received it because the Reality of Him will cause them to rise above and beyond *self*."

Alexis watched me silently for a moment, while the birds went twittering about on his person and the cats continued to sleep unself-consciously.

"I am amazed," he said finally, "that, knowing this, you committed suicide."

"Why amazed? What could *I* do about it except to have myself considered a crank and a meddler? It would have taken a miracle, Alexis, and I was too barraged on all sides to await any miracles!"

"But — *suicide*, Hellbent? Such a drastic step? Surely others on this Earth are disillusioned, too. Surely — "

"Then they are made of sturdier stuff than I, or they want material existence more than I. And I would not call forty years drastic, Alexis. It took me that long, that much of 'life,' to decide death (or, I hoped, peace) was better. Remember that for the last ten of those forty years I had Believers displaying their personalities on the one side, and Della on the other — "

"Ah, yes, Hellbent. What was her winning argument?"

I sighed heavily. "The sun is high now. Why don't the cats climb down and prowl? Why don't the birds go look for food? I remember they used to wake me at four in the morning in such weather as this. Chattering and trilling and flying back and forth. And the cat across the hall — "

"They are not hungry," Alexis said quietly, lifting a sparrow on his forefinger to permit it to rub its bill against his cheek. "They are full. But — you are hedging again, Hellbent. What was the final argument?"

" 'There is still time.' *That* was the final argument. When all else failed, when I had refuted every other argument, then she would weep and plead, 'There is still time, Willful. You can denounce this madness and it will melt away like a bad dream. Otherwise — otherwise — we will be apart forever! *Think* of it! Non and Vicie and I — away from you. . . . I know you are angry with me right now. I know I have used underhanded means of appealing to you. But wipe all that away and only think of the one fact neither of us has ever been able to bear. Out of all beings in all the Earth, Willful, only you are truly a part of me. Only I am truly a part of you. Conceived and nurtured in the same womb, inseparable since that very instant, soulfully affixed one to another . . . Willful, I can't bear it, I can't bear it! Please, while there is still time, break away from this nightmare and come back to me . . .'"

I broke off, my voice ragged. Alexis started to speak, but I said quickly, "Oh, I know that we are not supposed to love relatives more than Him. But loving Him more than her meant dwelling with *them*. And — I didn't give in all in a minute. In fact, I never even told her that I had given in at all. I refuted even that argument. I wept, too, and I said, 'Then you come *my* way. You believe and accept, Della. Between the two of us, we can convince Non and little Vicie. Do you think I can bear the thought of you in hell? You come my way . . .'"

"Yes? Yes, Hellbent?"

"She became very angry, I'm afraid. She drew away from me and crossed the room and said very coldly, 'Don't you start that hell-fire nonsense with me! I've heard evangelists by the score use fear to convict people of sin, but I know a little bit about *Him*, too, and I have yet to read a passage in the Guide Book wherein *He* employed those tactics! He had more to say about the self-righteous bigots you invite me to amalgamate with than He did about 'sins' those hucksters alternately cry and croon over! I am not afraid of what lies below, but I tremble when I think of what faces us above! Our parents and all their relatives and all those who have driven you to anguish since you made this foolish decision! I simply could not bear it! Nothing of the Guide Book shows in any of them. Indeed, the very opposites prevail. *He* never attempted to frighten people! Even Paul, who had committed infamous sins against Him, was simply made to see Him as He was. No, Willful. I will never come your way! Never inoculate such infantile gabble into another conversation with me

137

as long as you live! I will never change! *Never!*" And so . . ."

Alexis nodded solemnly. "You can tell me the mechanics of it along the way," he said. "Right now, we had better get started."

He shifted his position, but the birds only fluttered and maintained their various footholds. "Now, now," he said softly. "It is time for me to be off." One by one he picked up the birds and sent them out through the window. A few darted away, glinting in the sun for several yards. Some settled on twigs and branches, like colored bulbs, slowly going out.

Finally he picked the reluctant cats up and set them in the two opposite corners, one on either side of me.

"Now we are ready to go," he said, and instantly we were on the sidewalk below. We had walked only a few paces when the gray angora came down the tree yowling and streaking faint light. Directly behind it came the tiger, snarling and hissing. Across the street, behind a hedge and around a house they went. Alexis paused for a moment to watch them. Finally he wagged his head lamentably and we moved on. "It does not take long," he observed, "to lose touch."

CHAPTER 24

WE STARTED IN THE GENERAL direction of the school, and excitement cropped into my voice when I asked, "Will she be there today, Alexis? Will I be able to see her?"

"Yes," he said, walking with his hands clasped behind him as usual and with his face tilted slightly downward — though he seemed to see everything. "Vicie will be in school, and you will see her. On the way, however, there are a couple of details I should like clarified. We have discussed the pros and cons of your not actually becoming a church member from all sides save one. That is simply this. If you were honestly so appalled by the interpretations and tactics of Believers (and I am now convinced that you were) that you could not, for your own sake, join permanently with them, does it not stand to reason that you might have joined for *their* sakes? Since you and Della were steeped in religious practice and you then went on to become versed in Guide Book knowledge and understanding, is it not logical that, forgetting yourself, you might have helped *them*? That you were, in fact, needed by them?"

I wanted to grimace. "Alexis," I said sharply, "you drive a hard bargain! If you are not poking fun at me (and I am willing to concede that you also are sincere), then you already *have* the answer to that. I told you I nursed an ulcer, that I was a nervous tangle, and that they would not *listen* to me.

139

Sometimes I thought that if He appeared in Person, they would have gone right on about their boggling, browbeating and balking!"

"But He did leave His peace with you."

"But He left it when the world was far less complicated and the church far less shivered!"

"Now you know that is utter nonsense, Hellbent. He is the same yesterday, today and tomorrow. Be sensible enough to use the sense He gave you on His behalf."

"Are you trying to make me ashamed and guilty, Alexis?"

"I am trying to make you see that He will do just the opposite. He does not want your condemnation. He wants your happiness. But in order to receive the peace He has for you, you must first give Him obedience."

"That sounds like the logic of Even Swap."

"Not at all, and you well know it. For everything He takes He gives back many times magnified. But first, *you* must give. And peace comes when you are in accordance with His will. Do you think you were?"

"Apparently not, since you put it that way. But neither do I see that I could have done things differently. Do you?"

"You are convinced, then, that you did what He wanted you to do? He wanted you to commit suicide?"

I thought about it for a moment. Then I ventured, "Well, *He* did. . . . That is, He gave up the ghost."

"Giving one's life and taking it are two different things."

"All right, I was out of His will and I murdered myself. Is that what you want me to say?"

"I want you to say nothing except what you feel is true. Do you feel that is true?"

"Alexis, you seem to forget I have no desire to go above to dwell anyway, so what difference does it all make? If I were in His will, if I murdered myself, if I tell the truth — what does it matter? If I am a rotten egg, so much the better! Toss me out!"

"I see," he said. "It still comes back to that. Very well.

140

We have a lot to accomplish. Let us begin with the details of your suicide."

"What do you mean 'we have a lot to accomplish'? You continually talk and act as if we were keeping to some kind of schedule. If you intend to pressure me into changing my mind – "

He waved an impatient hand. "I am no evangelist, Hellbent. You need not be perpetually suspicious of me. Your free will is still very privately your own. As to the schedule, we can get to that later. Right now, be on with your suicide. You felt you were beset on all sides and had to come to the conclusion that further existence on Earth was pointless. Is that right?"

"Yes, that was part of it. I had also concluded that I did not want a continuation of dwelling with creatures like Bully Rude, Sharp Distinction, and my own disavowed tribe. No glorification including free will could polish the rough edges off them and make rubbing shoulders eternally less than extremely painful, to my way of thinking. I wanted to be done with them once and for all, and I wanted a chance to be near the only three people I love. After weeks of thought and deliberate planning, I decided that suicide offered the best solution. It would remove me from the present misery and confusion, and it stood the greatest chance, of any sin I could call to mind, of setting me in bad estate with Him. It, by its very nature, allowed no confession.

"I would leave Earth in a state of unconfessed sin. I even hoped it would give the aspect of a dash of idolatry since, as you suggested, I was putting my desire to be with Della, Vicie and Non ahead of being with Him. But apparently He saw through that because it was really quite obvious that if I had ever been able to put anything else ahead of Him, I would gladly have done so. And if ever I had been able to stop believing, I would not have had to go to such lengths to turn Him against me!"

141

Alexis shook his head and grinned. "'When I became a man,'" he quoted gently, "'I put away childish things . . .'"

"All right!" I barked. "So it wasn't a very bright idea and it didn't work! Do you have to be cute about it?"

"Cute!" he said. "Cute? I? Let me remind you that I have taken on this symbolic form for your benefit, Hellbent. To keep from terrorizing you! It might also do well for you to remember that even *He* took on a form such as yours so that you could learn from Him. You humans cannot seem to comprehend much beyond your own basic ingredients and therefore must be reached through those means! Cute, indeed!"

"Oh, you need not flash and spark and threaten to burst forth like a Roman candle, Alexis. I know I am stupid and wayward and foolish and belligerent. If I ever doubted that, I certainly had it pointed up to me when I botched my own suicide! I had planned everything so carefully and then — But what does it matter? You know what happened."

"I know," he said, confining himself to a steady glow, "but I should like to hear your version of it. Also, since leaving Earth separated you from people you found intolerable, did it not likewise separate you, for the time being, from those you loved? In other words, did you not feel it worth being with *them* to be with Della, Vicie and Non?"

"But it was not quite that simple, Alexis. Leaving Earth did separate me from loved ones, yes. But if I had risked continuing to live, I might have passed away suddenly in a state of grace! I couldn't risk *that!* It was better to forcibly remove myself and leave in a state of sin."

"But all those passages you knew which stated clearly that your condition in Him was not retractable. . . . 'He that believeth . . . shall not come into condemnation.' 'Neither shall any man pluck them out of my hand . . .'"

"I know, I know. But I was desperate, don't you see?"

"Well, then, what means did you decide upon?"

"I finally decided an automobile accident was most logical."

"Logical! But I should have thought — "

"Oh, I cast about for days, Alexis, even after that decision was made. My mind scurried from one alternative to another, every way out from putting a gun to my temple to the woman's trick of gulping down an overdose of sleeping tablets. All the obvious ways were too obvious. I didn't want Della to feel guilty about my death, so the best way was to make it look accidental."

"But what a risk! Supposing she, thinking it *was* accidental, later became a Believer? You might still be in opposite places!"

"Not Della," I said. "Della was always the stronger one. When she said no to Him, she really meant it."

"You did not even leave a note, then?"

"No. I simply selected a large, round oak — much like the one that fell on you — and pushed the accelerator to the floor."

"Dear, dear," said Alexis. "It does seem that drowning might have been less messy."

"It would have been. But it would also have been more obvious. I have never been the athletic type. I thought about stepping in front of a truck or a train, too, but that would have involved other people. I had to do this thing alone and sensibly."

"Ah, yes," said Alexis. "As you have done everything else. So? You selected an unyielding timber, drove directly into it at top speed — and then what?"

"And then I continued to live, dismembered, demented and gory, for six miserable hours!"

"Six?" asked Alexis.

"Exactly. You see, I planned the thing to happen at nine in the morning on my way to a book shop in a nearby town."

"You told Della you were going?"

"Yes. It was my day off, and she knew I liked to browse."

"But did it never occur to you that you might not die instantly?"

"I didn't think I could fail! I had had the motor gone

143

over. I had practiced picking up speed when the road was deserted. I just don't see how in the world — "

Suddenly he looked very expressionless. But he only said, "Yes, Hellbent? So what became of you?"

"Well, it seemed a police car had spotted me. I faintly recall hearing their siren. At any rate, they arrived minutes after I collided with the tree, summoned an ambulance and what was left of me was extricated and removed to a hospital."

"I take it you were in severe pain?"

"So much of it, all over, that I seemed dipped and drenched and could only find relief by babbling incoherently. My mouth seemed to be the only working part of me!"

"I see. And when you arrived at the hospital?"

"I remember that a student nurse fainted when she saw me. I remember that another one groaned and said, 'What if he should live — ?' And still another, 'God have mercy!' They worked over me for three hours, until noon. I remember uttering indistinct thoughts all the while. Finally they wheeled me into a room alone and, for a time, I heard their voices outside in the hallway. 'So what if it was a suicide? Leave the poor guy alone. To blazes with your newspaper and your police reports. What does he care what you write or record? It makes no difference what he said! They say all kinds of things. . . . You certainly may not take any pictures!' And then they cleared the way and let Della and Non in to see me. Incidentally, Alexis, I am sure it was no 'act' she put on at the graveside, as Cousin Rational suggested. She nearly fainted when she came into my room . . ."

"I know it was no performance, Hellbent. But go on."

"Well, I felt so sorry that I had bungled so badly that all I could seem to do for the next three hours, from noon to three in the afternoon, was explain and apologize! My tongue ran on and on. . . . Sometimes I realized a bit of what I was saying and tried to stop it, but I was helpless! It was almost as if — as if — *He had turned His back on me!*"

"But — that was what you wanted, was it not?"

144

"I thought I did — I'm sure I do! But, right then I wasn't so sure. . . . And they all just stood there staring down at me. . . . Della and Non, two doctors, two nurses. I wanted to see Vicie, but they wouldn't let me. I got the idea that I was too horrible for her to see. Somehow I thought wildly, 'This is what I get for once displaying willingness to never look upon her . . .' Finally a nurse wiped the blood from my mouth, and I died. That is, I passed from death to life. It happened so quickly! I breathed a last breath, I heard Della sob aloud, and then I was in the outer office of the High Registrar!"

Alexis nodded, smiling gently, but with sadness around his eyes. "If only humans would know this before it is too late, Hellbent. But, tell me. In your babblings I take it you confessed the entire plot to Della and Non?"

"I am afraid I did. So, now that they know, Alexis, they will surely join me in hell."

"Did Della say nothing at all during those last three hours?"

"She wept and swooned alternately, Alexis. They had to keep reviving her. Once, when she tried to speak, the doctor said, 'It's all right. Don't try. He wouldn't understand you anyway.'"

"And Non Regenerate?"

"His concern was mostly for Della, as it should be. Besides, with his way of looking at things, he undoubtedly felt that the doctor was right. The fragment of me that remained would not be capable of receiving communication."

"I see. It was probably for Della's sake, then, that the funeral was held the next day. The next morning. Closed coffin."

I stopped and stared at him. "The next morning? Do you mean — because I was so badly torn asunder. . . . But that means that, day before yesterday, we attended my funeral luncheon so that, actually, *we started our pilgrimage on the afternoon of my death?* And when I joked with the Chief

145

Counselor about formaldehyde — it was actually happening? This, then, is the third day after my — departure . . ."

"Yes, Hellbent. The third day." He looked somber.

"Alexis!" I said with sudden alarm. "Is this the *last* day?"

He stood very still and looked at me. In the distance a train whistle sliced through the silence. A dog growled. A mother scolded her child.

Finally Alexis said, "This is the last day, Hellbent."

"Then if I do not sufficiently prove my case by the end of today . . ."

"Three o'clock this afternoon."

"Exactly three days and three nights?"

"Exactly."

"But — " I began frantically, "what if I have not succeeded in convincing you? All along you have spoken of it as 'proving my case,' 'a score for my side,' but is it really that way? How do I stand, then? How do I add up? Alexis, *please!*"

He drew a deep breath and said, "It adds up exactly as you want it to add up, Hellbent."

"Do you mean I am closer to hell than to — "

"Is that the way you want it?"

"Oh, yes, Alexis, *yes!*"

"Then that is the way it is."

I cried out with a loud voice, dancing and twirling through the air with my vacuity. "I win! I win! I'm going to hell!"

But then another thought struck me and I fell in beside Alexis as he trudged solemnly along. "*Six hours,* Alexis? From nine in the morning until three in the afternoon? But that's exactly how long *He* suffered! That sounds like — almost as if . . . Would He do that to me, Alexis?"

"I am only a ministering spirit, Hellbent. I do know that He has gone to great lengths to convince men."

"But the three days and the three nights in which to prove my case! 'As Jonas was three days and three nights in the whale's belly, so shall the Son of man be three days and three

146

nights in the heart of the earth!' 'Also He went and preached unto the spirits in prison!' Is that it, Alexis? Is that it?"

"Is what what?"

"Well, He descended into hell and preached to the lost souls, didn't He? Does He give you the same length of time to deal with me that He gave Himself to deal with them?"

He plodded on, his eyes straight ahead. "What does it matter, Hellbent?"

I thought about it for a minute and then I laughed. "You are quite right. What *does* it matter? I shall see Vicie and Della and Non. I shall know that all is well. Then I shall be released — "

But I stopped abruptly and stared at the skirt of his garment.

"Alexis," I said, "you have a little spot of dirt on you! How can that be? It *looks* like dirt and yet it seems to move about . . . Here. Let me see." But instantly it was off him and on the ground!

"Never mind, Hellbent. It is only your shadow."

I gasped aloud. "My *shadow!* But I have no body so how in the world — "

"That's how, Hellbent. 'In the world.' "

"But it is no bigger than the head of a pin! In fact, a *small* pin! Do you mean I am no bigger than that? My spirit — or whatever it is that now compels me — is that tiny?"

"Whatever now compels you," he said evenly, "is that tiny."

"But I never cast a shadow before! Why should I suddenly — "

"Is it not obvious, Hellbent? Have you not said yourself that you are closer to hell? Farther away from the Light? But let us not dawdle, please. We are nearing the school."

I came along silently then, but the spot danced before me like a beckoning playmate with mischief in mind.

147

CHAPTER 25

THE BELL HAD NOT YET RUNG when we came onto the grounds. Like spokes of a wheel the sidewalks came together at the main entrance, and each spoke was an aisle filled with laughing, chattering youngsters.

"How old is she?" asked Alexis.

"Twelve," said I, brim full of anticipation. "She is in the sixth grade. A good little student, too. Her hair is dark like Della's and her eyes are bright blue. She should come from the west, I think. Della and Non bought a house in the newer addition. She has lots of friends. Della dresses her in all the latest fashions and permits her to entertain as often as she likes. . . . But look! There she is! See her? See her, Alexis? The little girl in the plaid skirt and the blue sweater!" I left Alexis' side and went swiftly across the grounds and out past the road to the path beyond. "Vicie!" I said, choked with happiness. "Vicie-darling, it's Uncle Willful!"

But Alexis was immediately beside me. "She can neither see you nor hear you, Hellbent. Even your shadow is too insignificant for her to notice."

"But — is there no way — ?"

"None whatever. You know that."

We followed along beside her for several steps and then I said, "Alexis, the air is very warm, isn't it? School will be out very soon. They should be having final exams right now.

Why does she quake like that? She has a wool sweater on. Surely she can't be cold . . ."

But even as I spoke she crossed her arms and hugged her small body. She looked as if her very teeth were chattering!

Alexis watched it, too, and his face was overflowing with compassion, but he did nothing.

"Alexis," I pleaded, "can't you touch her? Can't you warm her? Reassure her? She looks so little and sick! Can't you — "

"No, Hellbent. I am assigned to you."

"But that doesn't even make sense! Why isn't one of you assigned to her?"

He turned and looked at me with mild surprise. "Why should one of us be? Did you not say she was twelve? And quite bright? Should she not have heard of Him, then? But you yourself said that she would go to hell and that was what you wanted — "

"I see!" I said disgustedly. "You are a closed group, is that it? Pretty exclusive, eh? Then why do you trouble with me?"

His eyes widened and his shining brows drew up. "I won't," he said, "after three o'clock this afternoon. But until then you are still my charge. But let us get off this nonsense and get back to the child. You say she is popular. Where, then, are her friends? Surely after such an experience as your passing she should have little friends to comfort her."

I noticed for the first time how terribly alone she seemed. Other children were clustered in small talkative groups, but Vicie went by herself.

"Do none of them live near her?" Alexis asked. "Do they live in some other section of the town?"

"Why, no! There are lots of children in her neighborhood. She usually walks with five or six. They meet at her house, as a matter of fact."

"Well," said Alexis, "perhaps she went on without them this morning."

149

"She wouldn't do that. She's a very loyal little thing. Also very gregarious."

But then we crossed the street and came upon the grounds again. There, grouped ahead of us, was her little mob.

"There they are," I said. "They must have gone on without her . . ."

Vicie saw them, too, and she began to shiver all the more. They stood blocking the sidewalk, staring at her, so that she had to go out around them. When she did, they tittered and giggled.

"Sorry we can't play with you anymore," one little snip said with singsong sarcasm. "But my folks feel that enough is enough."

"It's one thing," another chimed in, using the same tone, "to be a — *what you are* (and here they all paused to snicker appreciatively) — but quite another to be a maniac!"

"Who knows what you might do?" a third one suggested. "With a father who goes beserk and commits — "

Vicie started to run. Casting her glance from side to side, she ran from them as if looking for a hiding-place — like a small frightened animal. Other youngsters turned and stared after her. I let out a hoarse cry and pursued her myself. Alexis was right beside me. She came, breathless and frantic, to the main entrance, but the teacher on guard at the door looked at her strangely and said, "Sorry. You have to stay outside until the bell rings."

The teacher continued to stare, her eyes curious and penetrating. Vicie backed away and cowered against the outside wall. She looked like the embodiment of innocence facing a firing squad!

"Alexis," I croaked, "*do* something!"

"Do something, Hellbent? Or *undo* something?"

"Help her! Comfort her!"

"I told you. I am assigned to you."

"Are you going to stand there and argue over a few hair-splitting details? She isn't that old! That she no longer war-

150

rants a guardian angel! Have you no heart? Are you all just glitter and obedience? How can you let this happen to her?"

But he looked at my torment without flinching. "The question is," he said finally, "how could you?"

"I don't know what you're talking about!" I snarled. "I didn't let this happen to her! I didn't tell those snobbish parents to —"

"But you gave them just cause," he reminded. "Did you think they would praise you for it? Did other humans praise your parents for what they did to you? Did they befriend you and Della for what your parents were? Sins always find you out, Hellbent."

Another batch of youngsters walked past Vicie, whispering and pointing. She turned her face away, toward the red bricks.

"This is no time for sermons!" I choked. "Can't you see she's cringing with shame? Don't you think I know what that feels like?"

"But apparently you forgot. Or you would not have brought this upon her."

"I didn't bring it on her! That is — I didn't mean —"

But now her little mob had made its way up to the door beside her. One of them, clad in pink, stepped a pace away from the others and said haltingly, "Vicie? It wasn't my idea for us not to be friends anymore. It's just that my folks — and all of theirs, too — it's just that — well, you know. All that stuff in the newspapers. And he *did* confess to doing it on purpose. And if that sort of thing runs in the family. . . . And everyone knows you're his daughter . . ."

Suddenly Vicie screamed. She doubled her fists at her sides and shrilled, *"Leave me alone!"*

The girls backed away and the teacher came all the way outside and took Vicie by the arm and said, "Now see here! We don't stand for shenanigans of that sort around here! You may be notorious to the rest of the county but in this place

151

you'll behave normally and decently or the principal will hear about it! Is that clear?"

She released the child with a jerk and stalked back to her post. Vicie stood helplessly against the building turning her face one way and then the other, tears sliding down her cheeks.

"Why doesn't she just go home?" I rasped.

"What would be the good of that, Hellbent? She is required by state law to attend school."

"But not yet! Not *yet* . . ."

"Will time make the facts go away? Apparently the facts surrounding her birth did not fade with time."

"Will you stop coughing up the past to me? Will you stop acting so sanctimonious? You talk as if I deliberately plotted to hurt this child! It wasn't my fault at all! I had it all worked out to the last detail! It was *His* fault! *He* was the one who interfered! If He had just let me die — if He hadn't caused me to burble all those hours . . ."

A batch of young boys walked past Vicie. "Well, well!" one of them quipped smartly. "If it isn't the little girl with the little curl right in the middle of her uncle's head!"

The others guffawed and slapped him on the back and they went on down the walk gossiping about the condition of the car — and my body. Vicie cowered with humiliation, and an agony beyond mere tears of remorse twisted and contorted me.

"All right!" I moaned. "It is my fault! I would never have done it if I had known it would end like this! Help her, Alexis! Please help her!"

"I have told you, Hellbent. I cannot. As you have said, she is beyond being a little child. She is old enough to think and reason. She must make her own decision about Him. I cannot help it if she has not been properly instructed. That was your commission and you failed."

"Do you mean she will go to hell?"

"But you wanted her to!"

"But — that is — *not yet,* Alexis! Not here on Earth — like this!"

"But you brought it upon her, Hellbent! If you had left things as they were, if you had stayed here with her, none of this would have happened. Your violent action only gave vent to undercurrent whispers that would otherwise never have erupted!"

"I — I can't undo it — "

"Of course not. It is too late for that."

"But she needs a comforter — "

"Of course she does. And He sent One."

"But how can I — ?"

"Don't *you* know?"

"But Della and Non — "

"We are talking about Vicie. Just about Vicie. Which do you think is worse? This life without Him, or eternity with Believers?"

Somehow I was sobbing. Dry, hard sobs. "What have I done? What have I done? I only thought — I only thought — *of myself!*"

Though I had no body, I had the sensation that Alexis' hand was on my head. "There, there," he said. "Let us go on. But first, look up, Hellbent. The school bell is about to ring."

I looked up toward Vicie and I saw a little girl dressed all in white come up close to her, and they seemed to be talking. I moved away quickly to hear them.

"It's all right," the little girl in white was saying. And now she put an arm about Vicie's shoulders. "It doesn't make any difference what they say. You mustn't pay any attention to them. They don't know any better. We must remember to pray for them. I will be your friend. And I will tell you about my very best Friend. Once you know Him, it won't hurt so bad. You see, a long time ago in Bethlehem . . ."

153

And suddenly the bell rang and the other children ran helter-skelter, pushing and shoving to get at the door, but Vicie and her new little friend disappeared serenely inside the building, talking and nodding with their arms about each other as if they were entirely alone.

I stared after them until the grounds became quiet and deserted. Then I turned to Alexis and said, "What does it mean? Who was that child? Was she — "

Alexis smiled. "No, she was not one of us. Your eyes must have been blurred. Though she has one of us to guard her. Her name is Dulce. She is your Cousin Hasty's niece by marriage."

"She's one of *them?*"

Alexis wagged his head. "You must remember, Hellbent, that your parents' relatives *did* attend your funeral — on very short notice. So did many of the members of the various churches you attended — though you had no knowledge of their presence."

"What is that supposed to prove? That blood is thicker than water?"

"No. That spirit is thicker than blood. You see, for all the squabbles, the foundational unity is astounding. In fact, miraculous."

"Alexis, you have got me at one very weak moment and caused me, somehow, to transmit an unuttered prayer to Him for Vicie, but don't get over-confident and think you can chicane me into — "

"I would not think of such a thing, Hellbent! If hell is what you want, I will not be the one to stand in the way. However, I am glad that little Vicie — "

"Alexis," I interrupted, "if the other child did have one of you guarding her, why couldn't I see him?"

"Your eyes are not open to the others. Only to me."

We were walking away from the school grounds now. Back to the main walk and beneath a canopy of maples.

"Alexis," I said again, "will she be all right now? Will she

154

really be all right? I mean, the other little girl, Dulce, will she tell her about Him? It doesn't seem fitting for a child to go to hell. Would you really have permitted that? Would He?"

"It is written, Hellbent, 'The son shall not bear the iniquity of the father.'" And he would say no more.

CHAPTER 26

WE PROCEEDED NORTH ALONG THE highway and then cut off to
the west on a gravel road. A flock of starlings flew overhead,
dipping low to freckle the earth with their shadows. The sun
was very warm now, making Alexis so bright when it shone
upon him that I could hardly bear to look directly toward him.
I looked, instead, at my little black shadow and wondered at it.

Finally I said, "Alexis, on the first afternoon we met you
said, 'What you are evolves out of what you were.' Though
I argued at the time that I would not overlook Believers'
behavior on those grounds, I do admit that I suffered for my
parents' sins. Still, you intimated that Vicie would not suffer
for mine . . ."

"She will suffer for yours, Hellbent, as long as she is on
Earth. He can dilute that suffering, however, as you have seen.
I spoke primarily of eternal suffering. She will not be judged
by Him for what you have committed. Unless, of course, she
should choose to use your sins as a basis and excuse for her
own. That is, to wallow in self-pity and thereby go astray."

"Did I do that, Alexis? Is that what you're saying?"

He sent me a glance. Not a full look. Just a glance,
bright and blinding. "I heard you confess to Him that you
thought only of yourself, Hellbent."

Sudden disgust poured through me. "Honestly, Alexis," I
said impatiently, "at this late date do you still have to turn
everything I say into a verbal spanking?"

156

"But, Hellbent, you asked me — "

"Well, I shouldn't have! Let's talk about something else!"

We went several yards in silence then. Finally Alexis said, "Hellbent, you seem to become more touchy as the minutes pass by. Also more resentful toward me. Being the reasonable Presence you are, do you not think that since you refuse to excuse other Believers' behavior on the grounds that their upbringing helped to make them what they are, you should likewise, in all honesty, refuse to excuse your own? You maintained that the doctrine of Christianity is, in itself, an education which necessarily causes the Believer to change and expand. So then no one, once he believes and accepts, has a right to lean upon his past as if it were a magnet holding him back from improvement."

"I didn't lean upon my past in that way," I said crossly. "I was willing to forgive and forget, but everywhere I went I saw only duplicates of my parents' relatives, or more advanced cases. Besides, I have told you it's too late to go on hashing it over now. You said it was up to me, and I have told you my choice. It's over and done with, and now I am only biding my time until you release me. Now that you know the full story of my life, you must have felt my arguments justified or you would not have agreed to let me go."

"Hellbent," he said, "you do not seem to understand even now. *I* do not 'let you go.' I am only — "

"I know, I know! A ministering spirit! Can we talk about something else, Alexis? Where are we going, anyway?"

"You wanted to see your grave, I believe."

"Oh. We're on our way to the cemetery?"

"Yes."

"But I also want to see Della and Non. Will there be time for that, too?"

"Yes, Hellbent. Plenty of time."

And then I laughed. "Of course! I forgot that I will at least spend eternity with *them*, won't I?"

He refrained from answering, and I supposed that it did

not set too well with him to lose a case. Although he had said that my outcome would in no way impinge upon his happiness.

I went on watching my shadow for a time and then I said, "How *can* I be that small? I *feel* bigger than that . . ."

"That is because you are inside yourself, Hellbent, that you feel big. If you came outside, you would see how small you are."

"But I was bigger than that on Earth!"

"Of course. You were filled with Him."

"You mean — I emptied Him out — sort of?"

"Yes. Bit by bit, you are doing that."

"And I began to cast a shadow when His light left me? But then why do Believers cast shadows on Earth while they live here?"

"Because they still have a fleshly nature and are still subject to temptation within their spiritual nature."

"But when I shed my Earthly body and went up above, I was rid of all that?"

"All but a scrap of diabolical temptation, Hellbent: your wish to spend eternity in hell."

"And when that won out — "

But he became silent again, and I was content to leave it that way. Still, being no more substantial than a flea *was* a curious state in which to find one's self!

But by this time we had reached the cemetery, and I turned my mind to the expanse of green velvet grass marked neatly off by marble headstones.

"Do you have a family plot?" Alexis asked.

"No," said I. "There was so much scrapping and disagreement that each little branch purchased its own plot as far away from the others as possible. Some went to cemeteries in other towns. We had no occasion to buy any."

"Well, then," he said, "we shall look until we come to it."

"But what if it has no marker as yet?"

"We will know," he said, "one way or another."

The cemetery covered a small hill. Beside the main gate,

a road turned in at the edge and wound around, coming out at the opposite side to form a nearly complete circle. We started at the main gate and walked slowly to the rise, looking left and right for newly sodded graves. There were none.

When we came to the peak, I turned to Alexis to say, "Perhaps she chose some other — "

And then I saw Non's car parked at the foot of the hill on the back road. In the far left corner he and Della worked at clearing away the remains of some cut flowers and painstakingly planted geraniums. Della seemed to be daubing at her eyes now and again, and Non would pause to pat her shoulder and speak to her.

"Alexis!" I cried happily. "They're here!"

I left him and hurried down the hill to the corner of the cemetery but, as usual, he was right beside me when I got there.

"Della!" I cried, gyrating up and down until my little black shadow looked like a tiny bouncing ball. "It's me! It's Willful! Don't cry, dear! I'm all right, see? It's just a box full of spare parts there in the ground! I'm here! I'm fine! I'm going to hell! We can all go to hell together — "

"Blinding blizzards, Hellbent!" Alexis interrupted. "If you never cease clamoring, you shall not be able to hear what *she* has to say!"

I settled down then and took notice of the fact that she was talking — or trying to, though Non had to keep patting her and saying, "Now, now, dear . . ."

"If only," Della wept, "he could have understood through his delirium. . . . If only he had not done this — we might all have gone on the same . . ."

"It's all right," Non said, drawing her head against his shoulder. "It will be all right. It's done now. We can't undo it. Don't cry, dear."

"If he had died instantly. . . . If I had never known . . ."

"It couldn't be helped, dear. It happened the way it happened and we must simply accept that."

159

"But if there were only something we could do for him . . ."

"There isn't. Nothing more now, dear. Vicie will be home soon for lunch. Come away and let us think of her. She must be told. Perhaps it will help. Come now."

But still she stood there, her hands wrung together, her face pale, staring at my grave through a blur of tears.

"In a way," Non offered then, "his condemnation was our salvation. Think of it like that. That it was all for a purpose."

But she only wept louder. "Oh, no! Not like that. For if I had hammered away a bit longer at him and if he had argued a bit more heatedly against my stubbornness — why, then . . ."

"No, Della. It would never have happened that way. Don't torture yourself. When you told him you wouldn't change, I am sure you really meant it."

"But — I don't think I did! Something inside me — some little splinter of faith from my childhood when we were still innocent to adult behavior — kept pricking at the inside of me . . ."

I began to be very perplexed. "Alexis," I said, "what *is* she talking about? I thought at first she was only grieving for me, but it sounds — "

"Suspicious?" whispered Alexis. "Then listen some more."

I turned my attention to Della in time to hear Non say, "You cannot go on like this, Della. You must think of Vicie. For her sake you must not dwell on Willful. You must remember what the Guide Book says, 'All things work together for good.' There is no other way. Leave it in His hands. Come now."

I gasped aloud. *"Non Regenerate!"* I cried. "Quoting the *Guide Book?* I don't believe it!"

But then Della was saying, "It all happened so quickly. When they called from the hospital, a sudden thrust went through me like a sword. I found myself thinking, 'I must tell him I am weakening to his way.' Then, when we arrived and

160

I learned how bad he was and when they told me the things he had been raving. . . ."

"Now, now, dear. Please don't get all worked up again. It's quite over and done with."

But she went on, as if she had not even heard him, "Then I knew for *sure* that I *had* to tell him! When I realized what a hideous thing it was to want hell so much . . . When I realized what a hideous thing *he* was for wanting it so much, for seizing the desire for it in his own two hands — the two hands on that steering wheel — " Her voice rose in hysteria, and he drew her against him.

"I tell you, Della, you will have a breakdown if you go on like this. It isn't worth it. You have your own life to live. You have to live for Vicie's sake now. She needs you more than ever. There is so much to do, dear. Think about where we'll start. Shall we change my name first of all? It will be quite simple, really. Just one letter. From Non to Now. How do you like that? Mrs. Now Regenerate?"

"Fine," she muffled against his shoulder. "If only Willful could know. If only I had been able to reason with him before he died, get him to confess — "

"But he did confess, dear. Over and over for hours."

"But to everyone but Him! Don't you see, Non? (I mean *Now*.) He needed to confess to Him . . ."

"But he already belonged to Him, Della. You know how sick we got of hearing about it. I can't believe one violent act — "

"It was more than that. He wanted the belief out of his life so badly that I think he worked at wrenching it loose like an infected limb. I have heard of those who willed themselves to the devil —"

"But there is nothing we can do, dear. It is all done. Please accept it. Try to think of it as I have told you. His downfall was our resurrection. There is no other way."

He tried to lead her away, but she moaned, "I threatened him! I said we would spend eternity apart unless he changed!

And now — and now — it will still happen! He will be in hell
and we will be — *up there*. . . . I can't bear it! I can't bear
what I have done! If only there had been some way of com-
municating with him at the last! If only we were all still together and could use our time to a better end!"

"It would be the same," he said. "Humans are very foolish
in that way. We would all be the same and you would be
threatening him with the opposite separation. It cannot be
undone, Della. Come away now. I insist that you come away."

He placed his arm firmly about her shoulders and moved
her toward the car. Still she kept glancing back at my grave,
her face contorted with misery. I stood there aghast staring
after them.

"I can't believe it!" I whispered. "They have become Believers? *Both* of them? My death was such an outrage that it
horrified them into believing?"

" 'How unsearchable are His judgments, and His ways
past finding out!' "

I turned upon him angrily then. "You knew it, Alexis?
You knew it all along?"

"Yes, Hellbent."

"Why didn't you tell me, then?"

"It would not have been ethical. You do not accept His
way because of another human. Another human may help or
hinder you, but ultimately you must accept or reject solely
because of Him."

"That's nonsense! I rejected Him because of her, didn't I?
And, besides, if it *is* true that I must accept or reject solely
because of Him, why, then you could say I did not really
reject *Him* at all! For I have never had any bones to pick with
His way, have I? Except that it should cause me to dwell with
badly behaved Believers —"

"Of which," Alexis said with amusement, "you are surely
not one!"

Resentment sharpened my voice to a keen edge. "It really
makes no difference, Alexis. I know Della very well. This will

162

gnaw away at the inside of her until she will probably go out and do the same thing I did! Don't worry. When she gets to thinking of eternity with all our parents' relatives —"

"You *thought* you knew her very well," he said quietly. "But even if you were right, she would never reach the point of doing what you did. He has already taken care of that."

And suddenly we were directly in front of Della as Now Regenerate helped her over a rough spot and down to the car. Alexis passed his hand before my line of vision and when he took it away I saw Della as though she were naked and had transparent skin — like a chart in a doctor's office. Her heart beat and her blood flowed and there, in her abdomen, I saw a growth. I had no sooner seen it than my sight became once more normal (for a Presence such as I), and she was again clad and making her way into the automobile.

I turned to Alexis and said all in haste, "What was *that?* I know very little about the human anatomy, except what I have had to research for various articles, but that looked —"

He nodded his head slowly.

"A tumor, Alexis?"

Again he nodded.

"But surely not —"

"Yes, Hellbent. Malignant."

"Malignant!" I croaked. "Surely you can't mean my beautiful Della is *dying* —"

"No," he said gently. "I only mean she is getting ready to leave this mortal shell and come at once, free and unfettered, into eternal joy."

"You make it sound so easy!" I said. "As if one would not writhe and writhe with torment —"

"But of course the extraction is sometimes painful. The thing is, pain is bearable — and death is most bearable of all! Just when you think you can stand it no longer, suddenly there is no more to stand and immediately you have crossed over. There you are, with all of eternity before you and sub-

163

lime happiness growing greater with each step you take closer to Him. That is our real aim and goal, you know."

"It sounds good," I said bitterly. "But you left out the part about the High Registrar and the Chief Counselor and the Individual Counselors *and* Rigid Pharisee, Mrs. Snob, Mrs. Insecure . . . Besides, Della will balk when she gets there."

"Possibly. Unless someone could be there to meet her. Someone she loved and trusted. But then, it is too late for all of that, isn't it? You have made your choice. Come along."

He started away, and I saw, too, that Della and Now Regenerate had driven off. I was compelled to follow at Alexis' side.

"What of Vicie and Now Regenerate?" I asked. "What will become of them after Della —"

"They will be fine," he said cheerfully. "You saw Regenerate's belief bringing peace and acceptance to his face. You heard the reassurance in his voice. He has always wanted a family, you said. He will do everything to make Vicie happy and secure — in every way. You need not give any of them another thought, Hellbent. And please stop lagging. We have one more stop. The last one."

"The last one?"

"Yes, Hellbent. The last one."

Sudden remorse spilled over inside me at the thought of all I had lost. "I am like Samson!" I cried. "In my death, He used me to accomplish what I would not accomplish in my life! Wretched fool! Wretched fool. . ."

"We must hurry, Hellbent," he said. "There is no time for that now."

I came along like a galley slave, the thought of hell no longer piquant and provocative, but only bleak and desolate.

CHAPTER 27

AND THEN I SEEMED TO PASS through a long tunnel which became narrower and narrower. It was very dark and at the tiny round opening at the very end of it I saw a small, flickering light — like a bulb dangling crudely from the ceiling, swayed by drafts and currents. Alexis was not with me. His little finger would have plugged the tunnel and filled it with such brilliant radiance that, in that confined area, would have blinded and agonized any occupants.

Terror and panic seized me. I heard voices at the end of the tunnel and, recalling the reversals preceding my descent, I trembled with fear of the unknown. "Alexis!" I cried out hoarsely, and my voice bounced against the sides of the tunnel and re-echoed again and again.

"I am out here," he said consolingly. "I can hear you, Hellbent. Do not worry. I will not leave you until you have safely arrived at your destination."

"You've put me down an ant hill!" I accused.

"Go along, Hellbent," he said gently. "We've no time to dally."

I knew that if I attempted escape, he would have blocked the outside opening. It was either stay in the tunnel, which sooner or later, I reasoned, would become clogged with such Presences as myself, or else go down and join the group at the other end. Stealthily, feeling my way with my hands against

165

the warm, dry wall, I moved step by step down to the end of the tunnel.

I emerged in what seemed to be a basement. It took a moment for my vision to clear, though I never did see everything clearly at once. Only one thing at a time and the rest of it in a haze. Like actors stepping to the middle of the stage and then retiring to the shadowy sidelines. The single bulb hanging from the ceiling was not moving at all, but only appeared to move as gusts of mist and smoke obliterated it now and again. The air was thick and stifling, pregnant with the odor of earth, tobacco and perspiration. The ceiling was very low and there were no windows. Heat and smoke and mist (which I recognized now as a kind of steam) seemed to emanate from the very walls, for there were no other openings.

I stood there blinking, trying to make out the still, gauzy forms in the room (for they had all become quite silent when I entered), and suddenly someone said, "Well, do sit down! The meeting has been held up long enough as it is!"

I turned my attention in the direction from which the voice had come and saw, glaring at me, a sharp-featured hag. "Sit down!" she cackled again. "Have you no respect? This is a worship service!"

I edged over to the splintery bench and sat down beside her. "Now pay attention!" she snapped, looking toward the front with an air of superiority.

"Oh, pay attention yourself!" a female voice in front of us shrilled. "You break up every meeting with that big mouth of yours!" She turned around, and I gasped. She was as obvious a portrayal of a harlot as ever I had seen. Her hair was brittle with red dye and her face, in that nebulous light, looked like a Halloween mask. Her dress was black and profusely decorated with fringe. Her face contorted and her arm reached out. It took me a moment of confusion to decide that she was smiling and beckoning. "You can sit by me if you wish," she said sweetly.

"Ha!" cried the Hag. "Sit by you, all right! Everybody

here knows what *your* game is! If you'd be a little more spiritual, we might be able to concentrate long enough to get through —"

"If *I'd* be a little more spiritual!" screamed the Harlot, getting to her feet. "Everybody knows why *you* sit in the back row! So you can fleece every newcomer in the hope of stuffing that corncob pipe one more time! You took the oath with all the rest of us that you'd swear off —"

"So did you!" said the Hag, rising to look her in the eye. "But I see that every man that comes in the back door —"

The Harlot reached out and slapped the Hag's face. The Hag pulled up the sleeves of her ragged sweater and grabbed a handful of the Harlot's red hair. They began to snarl and growl, a tangle of fists and claws and flailing limbs. I got to my feet and backed away. Somehow, I seemed to be backing toward the front of the room, up the center aisle. Someone tripped me and I fell on my back. Several of them laughed loudly.

"You had that coming!" said the red-faced fat man who stood above me. "But get up out of the way before I kick you, or we'll never get this meeting to order. Every time we settle down and try to get through, some new devil comes in and the fracas starts all over again!"

I scurried to one side for fear he would step on me, and he promptly went back and took the two women by the hair of their heads, cracked them soundly together and sat them down with a jerk. There followed a roar of applause and cheering, and then they all turned toward the front again. The Fat Man came wheezing back to resume his position on his bench and, seeing me there, said, "Get up out of the way, you fool, and go sit across the aisle!"

I got up to do as he said and perched gingerly on the end of the bench across from him. I was no sooner seated than a voice hissed in my ear, "You got a deck of cards and a little cash on you, brother?"

I turned quickly and a very personable young man with

thick wavy hair and very white teeth moved his hands supplely before my eyes. "I — why, no . . ." I said. "Sorry . . ."

His face at once became cruel and hateful. "Then what makes you think you can squat here, I'd like to know?" And he gave me a shove that sent me to the Fat Man's lap!

I thought the Fat Man would surely pulverize me, but he only laughed jovially and whispered, "Bring any food with you?"

But when I shook my head no, he sent me up the aisle sprawling. Several faces peered at me. One of them spit on me. I think he had consumption. Another picked me up by the neck and whispered raggedly, "Got a flask on you?" Then shoved me back down. I crawled a few feet on my hands and knees, uncertain as to whether it would be worthwhile to attempt standing. Then the voice of an elderly gentleman said kindly, "You can sit here, son. Beside me."

I looked up at the vacant spot he indicated and then carefully crept to a position beside him. "Now be quiet, son," he said, "and there will be no more trouble. Once we can maintain peace long enough to get through —"

A gavel sounded at the front of the room and, searching through the stench and vapor, I saw a man in priestly garb standing up behind a pulpit!

"Why," I whispered to the gentleman beside me, "you are all playing church!"

He turned to me smiling and said, "Son, you should not have said 'playing.' It infuriates me to be taken lightly." And then without another word he closed his hands about my throat and began strangling me while the others looked on and laughed! He twisted and turned and squeezed his hands together with all his might and, somehow, I remained the same — except that I was in a rather embarrassing, upside-down position through it all. At last he flung me away, while the others laughed still louder, and I realized that he was a murderer! A sweet-faced old murderer. But wholly incapable of killing again. Just as the Fat Man was incapable of eating, the Card Shark incapable of gambling, the Drunk incapable of drinking, the Harlot incapable of sex, the Hag incapable of chewing or smoking! It was a place housing the acme of physical frustration!

"I — I don't know where I am!" I said to all of them in general. "I didn't think I wanted to go above — that is, in the first place. And yet it seems — you call this a worship service. . . . I thought I came *down,* but possibly it was some underground passage leading *up —* "

"Do you mean," asked someone. "you had a *choice?*"

"Well, of course," said I. "Everyone has a choice."

"He's a liar!" said the Card Shark. "No one ever asked me!"

"Me, either!" said the Drunk. "Closest I ever come to anyone asking me was a woman with a tambourine who came around collecting. . ."

"I was asked," said the Murderer, "but it didn't seem worth it —"

"I went to church once!" yelled the Harlot. "They got up and moved away from me!"

"No wonder!" cackled the Hag, and then they all started fighting and scrapping again. It took quite a while before they settled down. The gavel finally did the trick. They sat, one by one, and faced the front. I seemed to have found a spot beside a polite, middle-aged woman.

"Those of us who were church members," she whispered, "have to set an example for the others."

"Then —" I began doubtfully, "you *are* a Believer —?"

"Oh, of course!" she said quickly. "We are *all* Believers!"

I stared at her. "Then I am in —?"

"Oh, my, no!" she said. "We are all Believers, but we believed *too late.* . . You see, once you come down here, there is no more doubting *Him!* We have it on Authority that He exists and that His way is the only way! The problem is — *establishing contact.* The Reverend up there in front knows the how of it better than any of the rest of us, being shepherd to one of the largest churches in the country. . ."

"But — if he was a shepherd — and you were a church member —"

"Well," she said, beginning to fidget, "if you're going to be that way about it. . ."

"But — I am not being any 'way' about it. I simply wondered —"

"Well, if you think you're better than we are . . . *That's* the way it was on Earth, you know. Some of those plain little churches came around preaching supernatural nonsense about believing and accepting, when we knew perfectly well that doing the nicest and kindest deeds —"

"But surely you know *now* —"

She shot to her feet and said loudly, "I demand that this trouble-maker be removed!" And she began to pommel the top of my head with her fists. At once the shouts and hurrahs began again. The Hag and the Harlot got into another tangle. The Fat Man reached over and belted the Drunk. The Murderer started in on the Card Shark. I could see these as I turned my head from side to side to avoid the blows, but there were many other struggling figures only partially visible in the filmy edges of the miasma. It took, once more, a long time getting them settled.

By the time the gavel sounded again, I was on the opposite side of the aisle and still nearer the front. A nervous man sitting next to me started to pick at me.

"Don't mind him," said a voice behind me. "He's a thief."

And another uproar began! "I'll thank you to mind your own stinking business!" the Thief hollered, turning to the woman in back of us. "If you hadn't been so busy breaking up your sons' marriages and worming money and pity out of them, maybe you'd have had a little time to believe before it was too late yourself!"

"That's right!" sided the Harlot. "She thinks that because

170

her sin didn't show she can sit up there in front and pretend to be closer to Him than the rest of us!"

"What would you know about it?" yelled the Hag. "Your sins were worse than mine and you sit up there ahead of me, don't you? All I ever did was bootleg a little corn whisky! Didn't even touch the stuff myself. Just ran a quiet little business so's my young'uns would have security. Sat on my own back porch and minded my own business —"

"Then why don't you try minding it down here?" cried the Harlot, reaching for her.

"Why don't *you?*" shrieked the Meddler, coming down the aisle to enter the battle.

"Why don't we just all sit down and shut up?" bellowed the Fat Man, taking a swing at the Murderer. "It's plain enough we're *all* down here because we were too busy at other things to listen to Him or believe Him —"

"It wasn't that way at all!" sniped the Card Shark. "Those who did know just never cared about those like me —"

"If you'd have come out of the back room long enough to see the light of day," said the Murderer, "you would have noticed signs all over, people on street corners, missions —"

"Listen who's talking about the 'light of day'!" laughed the Card Shark. "An old rabbit who spent his time hopping down alleys strangling people!"

"Don't laugh at me!" screamed the Murderer. 'I won't stand for —" He lunged at the Card Shark, who sidestepped, and grabbed, instead, the Drunk. The Drunk only laughed and permitted him to strangle away while he himself reached out and gave the Meddler a swat.

The gavel sounded again and this time I seemed to be standing in the aisle while they all took their seats. I turned then to the front and faced the Shepherd who looked strangely like a great auk standing there in his dark garb.

"I don't belong here!" I croaked. "I *am* a Believer! That is, I was even before I came down here! I never stopped believing! I spent years studying! The only reason I'm here

171

is because – because – *But I don't want to anymore!"* The words were harsh and cutting when they came through my throat.

The Shepherd only said, "Call me Reverend."

I looked at him and blinked. "No!" said I. "I can't! Because you *aren't!* If you had been –"

But then they all leaped up from their benches and started yelling and shaking their fists, some for me, some against me.

"Let him have a go at it!" said the Fat Man. "The Reverend ain't been doin' so hot –"

"Do not blaspheme!" said the Good Deed Doer. "The Reverend comes from one of the largest churches –"

"Yeah?" said the Drunk. "Then what's he doing down here? I say give this skinny little mutt a chance! We been here for years and so far all the Reverend does is pound the gavel and say, 'Call me Reverend!' He can't get through because he don't know *how,* see? If he'd known how –"

The gavel sounded again and some of them sat down. Others milled toward the front, shoving me along with them. I don't know what would have happened if suddenly the tunnel door at the back had not opened and, with a gust of clear, warm air, admitted a young man in what appeared to be a leather jacket. The whole crowd turned and concentrated upon him and he stood, exactly as I had, and strained to see around the room.

The Hag spoke first. "Sit down!" she said to him. "Can't you see this is a worship service? Sit down and pay attention!"

He seemed more reluctant than I had been. His eyes shifted about suspiciously.

The Harlot spoke up, "You can sit by me if you wish." Her voice was honeyed and she gestured and beckoned as she had to me.

"I ain't got none of the junk on me!" the young man announced angrily. "And I didn't steal it, neither! I was on my

172

way home after a legitimate purchase when these mugs grabbed me and knifed me in the back! Besides, I was going to swear off after this time, so why am I down here in this hole?"

"Well!" spat the Good Deed Doer. "If you think you're better than we are —"

"I had a daughter-in-law just like you!" said the Meddler. "Always shooting off her mouth! I don't see why my son never understood the favor I did him —"

"Got a flask on you?" asked the Drunk.

"Bring a deck and some cash, brother?" asked the Card Shark.

"Got a candy bar in your pocket?" asked the Fat Man.

"Come, son," said the Murderer. "You may sit by me. . ."

And then the gavel sounded and the Shepherd said in a monotone, "Call me Reverend. . ."

Suddenly I saw how it would be through all eternity. It would go on and on and on. They would never "make contact." They would quarrel and bicker and snarl and lash out. They would fight and attempt to kill, but they would live on and on, forever writhing beneath the anguish of their own personal frustration. The god each of them had put before Him on Earth was now just out of reach down here. Only the hunger remained, setting them on edge and sustaining the hope that each new arrival could bring fulfilment. And I, because I had yearned after an eternity free from Believers with terrestrial characteristics, was condemned to eternity with Believers possessing subterranean characteristics!

The words of the Chief Counselor rang in my ear: "Once condemned to hell, you could not howl and come back up here."

And still, knowing this, I somehow had to make a clean breast of it before Him. So, while the others pressed to the back, toward the Addict, and while the Shepherd stood woodenly clutching his gavel, I sank to my knees in the

173

aisle and cried hoarsely, *"My God, My God, why have I for-saken You?"*

There was an immediate stillness followed by weeping and gnashing of teeth. Suddenly the door to the tunnel was flung wide sending a shaft of light in from above.

"He established contact!" one of the women screamed, and then they all ran headlong toward the open door but, somehow, though they clawed and screamed and climbed over one another, none of them could seem to get through the open door!

I heard a voice say, "Come." And with joy leaping in my heart I walked through the mob, which seemed to be a mass of arms and legs twisted and knotted and helpless as intertwined reptiles, and entered into the foot of the tunnel.

CHAPTER 28

THE ASCENT PROVED FAR MORE difficult than the descent had been for I had grown in size and seemed to grow more with each step I took! The walls of the tunnel pressed in on me until I went from standing to stooping to going along on my hands and knees and, finally, *crawling!*

"I will never make it!" I shouted, hoping Alexis was outside.

"Hurry!" he said — though it was not much consolation that the voice was his for it seemed filled with concern. "The only way out is the way in which you went in — through your own effort!"

I began clawing wildly then. Inch by inch until my hands (for I seemed to have had them since I emerged in the pit below) were nearly at the edge of the opening.

"A little farther," he said. "One more good stretch . . ."

I tried but could not make it. My shoulders seemed to balloon until I thought I should strangle and die, lodged this close to escape.

"What is your first name?" Alexis asked impatiently. "Say it!"

"Willfully," I gasped. "*Will*-fully . . ."

"Do you want to come out or do you not?" he barked.

"*Will*-fully," I grunted again, straining with all my might. And then, when my arms felt as if they had left my shoulder sockets, my fingertips curled around the edge of the outside opening! I pulled until every inch of my body felt raw and bleeding from scraping on the sides of the tunnel. The hardest part came between the wrists and the elbows, for my hands were helpless and there was nothing I could hang onto or clutch. I braced my arms, V-shaped, against the outer edge, peeling off the flesh as I ejected my body a foot nearer the opening. Then my elbows were through and I bent them outward, stripping my upper arm to the bone as my shoulders edged forward.

At last my arms were out to the pits, but my ever-increasing shoulders pressed into my neck on either side until my eyes bulged and I felt as if my head would be forcibly popped off.

"*Pull*, Willful!" Alexis urged. "Pull quickly!"

I fanned both arms wide against the rocky outside and strained until my blood vessels seemed to burst, one by one, in my ears. Then, with one great, last agony of expulsion, my head and shoulders were through the opening! I scurried feverishly to extract the remainder of my being from the mouth of the tunnel which seemed to be closing like an iron claw. I was at last free and outside! The air was fresh and sweet and bright and cool. I saw Alexis standing there smiling, gently nodding his head.

"Alexis!" I choked. "My beloved friend! My help in time of need!" I reached out to embrace him, but suddenly I realized I had no arms at all! No legs! No head! In fact — I was incorporeal!

"But how — " I said. "When — where — "

Alexis laughed. "Come, Willful. Ask on the way."

We started off and I, free and airy and spilling over with delight, skipped and twirled. Though once I did pause to look back and, to my amazement, saw no tunnel-opening at all!

"What became of it?" I asked Alexis.

"It is still there," he said, "for those who will not permit

Him to give them a better place to spend eternity. They have to forget themselves long enough to listen to Him, you see."

"But," I said, remembering the pitiful tangle of limbs at the foot of the tunnel, "they *try* . . ."

"They try *now*," he corrected. "Now that it is too late."

We seemed to be going along at a brisk pace, and Alexis looked neither left nor right.

"But *I* was permitted to come out . . ." I said.

"Only because you believed before you went in. I was granted special permission to let you glimpse what you thought you desired, to show you that, like all the other things you thought you could substitute, it was only bitter disappointment. Also, if you had not really wanted to come out enough to bear physical death once more, you would not have escaped. You would have slipped back."

"Then — I really came very close to condemnation?"

"You had to want to come out more than you wanted to stay in."

"What became of the body I had? I am sure I had one . . ."

"That was the housing of all animal suffering, Willful. You shed it with the last of your diabolical desire."

I danced around and looked at the ground then. "My shadow is gone!" I said.

"Quite gone, Willful."

But then I thought of something else. Shamefully I admitted, "Alexis, I really thought the way it turned out to be down below was what it would be like up above . . ."

Alexis sent a bright smile in my general direction. "And now what do you think it will be like up above?"

"I think — I think — it will have none of that sort of thing in it at all!"

He smiled even brighter, nearly blinding me. "Anything else?"

"I think possibly that somehow — I don't know how, mind you — it will be the place I've always dreamed of. A place transcending personality differences . . ."

"Willful," he said, beaming until I could see nothing whatever except the fiery-white glare of him, "you are thinking much better thoughts."

I felt quite pleased. Not with myself, for I had done nothing. But quite pleased simply because he was pleased, and pleasure seemed to flow mutually between us like a warm, shining stream of light.

"Alexis," I said then, "am I larger now?"

"Much larger, Willful. Can you not feel it?"

"Yes, I think so. Though I feel so light and free. Alexis?"

"Yes, Willful."

"I know now what you meant about not feeling sad any more. The creatures in the pit, I mean. . . . I know they are there, but the time is past . . ."

"Exactly, Willful. You cannot quell the surge of joy within yourself, can you? Nor can it be permissible for the self-imprisoned to prohibit such joy. Otherwise the upper abode would not be the upper abode. It cannot be what it is if it has a taint of hell in it, can it?"

"I see," I said. "It all seems very clear now. Also it seems clear why the upper abode should not consist of any of the things I feared and dreaded. How could it and, as you say, be what it is? Also, you have helped me. So then, others can be helped, too."

Alexis turned to me and sparkled playfully. "You are quite ready to take all the rest on trust, then?"

"Absolutely! Only — will I never see you again? There must be so many and you will be so busy . . ."

"Would it make you sad never to see me again?"

"Of course not! *Nothing* can make me *sad!* Not anymore! But — my joy might be increased if once in a while — "

"I should not be a bit surprised," he laughed. "For eternity is immeasurable in Earth-time and fuses past, present, and future together in the upper abode. In that way, I shall always be with you if I have been a cause for happiness — "

"Oh, you have, Alexis! You've made me very happy!"

178

"*He* has made you very happy," he corrected gently. "I am only His instrument. However, we shall possibly meet in our own persons on occasion as well as commingling forever in His Person. Your joy will be increased. Of that I am sure."

"Alexis, are we going where I think we are going? Am I really, after all my wickedness, to have a second chance?"

"It is not a second chance, Willful. It is the same first chance. And it is really no 'chance' at all, for you made it a certainty when you believed and accepted. You might call your experience a kind of rededication."

"But I could have lost out . . ."

"Of course you could have lost out! *By choice.* For if there were no real losses and no real gains, then there would be no real choices, would there? But look! It is ten seconds to three!"

And with that we left off walking (for we had not been walking on Earth for several minutes, but in space) and were immediately above. In the near-distance I saw again the golden glow. The grayness from which we came shaded into clear, light blue. The blue into silvery, shimmering white. And beyond the white, gold emitting such light as to give itself a rosy overcast.

"We are right on time," Alexis said, smiling brightly on me. "Eternal joy, Willful."

"Thank you, Alexis," I said. "Thank you for everything! And — God bless you!"

He was leaving now, but he turned and beamed radiantly. "He always has, Willful! He always has!" And with one last wave he walked toward the golden horizon until the glittering whiteness of his raiment turned rose and then gold, and then even the phosphorescence flickering off in his wake became only flecks of gold dust, and he disappeared into the everlasting glory.

CHAPTER 29

No sooner had Alexis vanished into the eternal sunrise than I was seated once more in the outer office of the High Registrar. As before, there were other Presences like myself here and there about the designated space. Also as before, they chattered and worried and occasionally snapped at one another.

"I do wish they would hurry!" said Mrs. Impatient, twitching uncomfortably. "I was a long enough time dying in that miserable convalescent home. You would think they could at least use a little consideration up here."

"Hmmph!" said Surly Miser, sitting next to me. "Probably bled her husband dry before she kicked off."

"I heard that!" said Mrs. Impatient. "And I'll have you know that my husband, however slow he might have been, was never one to deny his family comfort. As long as we gave our fair share to Him, we were always blessed —"

"Oh, no!" groaned Miser. "Don't tell me I've got to hear that even up *here* . . ."

"Now, now," I heard myself saying, quite amused by it all, "it won't be at all like that. You shall have all of time, Mrs. Impatient. And you, Mr. Miser, shall have only to receive."

They both turned to stare at me, and, as they did so, a

180

strange realization flitted through my mind: Complete Trust, whom I had met on my first appearance in this office, had been on his second time through! *That* was why he had been so utterly reassured! Though possibly there were some few, some very few, who were ready to go directly on. I found myself wondering then, fleetingly, whatever happened to the other Presences who had been with me that first time. Possibly they had adjusted sooner than I. Possibly I would meet them again. Possibly — never. Though I doubted that. And I truly looked forward to the encounters.

But I had no further chance to ponder for the Receptionist materialized and said, "Mrs. Impatient, come this way . . ."

Mrs. Impatient rose and followed. They disappeared, half hidden in the mist, behind the iridescent door.

There was a rustle as several new Presences appeared and were seated. Then another came to sit at the opposite side of me. I recognized him at once and my being warmed with love and understanding. His name was Seriously Reluctant.

"You seem to be quite sure about everything," he said nervously. "Truthfully, I don't know how I came to be up here for election. Except that I believed. I didn't really *mean* to believe. And for years I got away without believing. But then, as time went by, and I watched all those crabs (mostly my own relatives) having a spat here and a tiff there, why, I couldn't help believing. I thought, 'Anything managing to continue and expand with all that going on inside it *must* have Him at the controls.' And so, I just *believed. . . .*"

"I know," I said. "I know. But don't worry about it. It will be all right. Really it will."

"It's easy for your kind to talk," he said rather grouchily. "You probably never had a doubt in your life!"

"Oh, I did," I said. "I'm sure we all did. But it doesn't matter now. He will make it all right. You'll see."

"I'd like to know how He's going to make it all right that I saved all my life and died before I spent any of it!"

inserted Surly Miser. "I'd like to know how He's going to make *that* all right!"

I felt my formless face smiling broadly. "Perhaps," I said gently, "the pleasure was in the saving. But it will make no difference now."

"Pleasure!" he snorted. "Going without the teeth I needed? Squinting to read my paper? Shivering all winter — "

But then the Receptionist appeared again and stood before him. "Mr. Miser, come this way . . ." And they were gone, around the end of the desk and beyond.

"*Will* it be all right for him?" asked Reluctant. "Or will he go on grousing all through eternity and I shall have to listen to him as I did to old Aunt Harpy . . ."

I could not keep from laughing aloud. "It will be all right for him," I assured Reluctant. "It will be all right for you, too. Simply trust and obey."

"But will we have no free will?"

I smiled even over this. "I am sure we will have," I said. "More and better than ever before."

But before he could question that, there was another rustle and two more Presences appeared. One of the others got up and took Surly Miser's seat next to me.

"I couldn't help overhearing you," she said in a middle-aged voice. "Frankly, I don't think too much freedom is a good thing. I have never approved of the questionable attire of many Guide Book characters, any more than I approve of stockingless legs, sleeveless dresses — "

"Tell *me* it'll be all right!" interrupted Seriously Reluctant with a sigh of disgust. "How can it be? When they can fly over and pick away at you even in a place like this — "

"It will be all right," I said, still smiling. "Take His Word for it." And then I turned to the female Presence and said, "I feel sure you will find it all to your liking, too, Mrs. Strait-Laced. I am sure each of us will have his mind above and beyond — "

But then the Receptionist was standing before me. "Mr. Heavenbound, come this way . . ."

Embarrassment skittered through me like an electric shock, so quickly that the sensation was a pleasure. I started to say, "There must be some mistake. I am Hellbent. Willfully Hellbent — for election."

But when the Receptionist's eyes met mine, I saw the mirth — clear and deep. There had been no mistake. My name had been changed for obvious reasons. I was an adopted son, already elect.

Merriment shone for an instant between us, like two sharing a great, secret joke. And then I arose and followed, doing a wee jig to give vent to the singing and laughter that swelled inside me until I like to choked from the anticipation of joy yet to come.